WHEN WE FLEW AWAY

A Novel of
ANNE FRANK
Before the Diary

ALICE HOFFMAN

WHEN WE FLEW AWAY

A Novel of

ANNE FRANK

Before the Diary

SCHOLASTIC INC.

ISBN 978-1-5461-7546-9

12 11 10 9 8 7 6 5 4 3 2 1   25 26 27 28 29 30

Printed in the U.S.A.   40

Originally published in hardcover by Scholastic Press, September 2024

This edition first printing, January 2025

Page 112, "I would not ask if conditions here . . .": reprinted courtesy of the
Archives of the YIVO Institute for Jewish Research, New York.
Page 132, "I have taken up the matter of your immigration . . .": reprinted
courtesy of the Archives of the YIVO Institute for Jewish Research, New York.

PUBLISHED IN COOPERATION WITH THE ANNE FRANK HOUSE

Book design by Elizabeth B. Parisi

How wonderful it is
that no one has to wait even a minute
to start gradually changing the world…
—Anne Frank

There is a day you never forget, the day the whole world changes.

When you close your eyes, light becomes dark, night never ends, beasts walk freely down the street, stars fall from the sky. You were young one second, and then you were far too old. You lived years in minutes and decades in weeks.

You wanted to travel, you wanted to grow up, you wanted to be beautiful, you wanted to fall in love. You wanted so much that your heart broke in half, but half a heart is better than none, and your heart is stronger than anyone would guess.

You remember everything.

You see the leaves turning green on the elm trees along the canals after the spring snow. Songbirds are rising up from the branches, and the bells over the bookstore doors are still ringing. There is a heron sitting on a balcony, a bird that is a sign of good luck. You are wearing two sweaters and a coat though the day is warm. When you see black moths rising from deep underground, you can barely breathe. In this moment, you suddenly realize you may not always be with the ones you love. Something is happening all around you.

This is when you understand that the story can change.

PART ONE

Little Sister
Amsterdam, May 1940

Once, there were two sisters. One was beautiful and well-behaved, and one saw the future and stepped inside it. One planted a rosebush, but the other one noticed that every white flower was turning red. One did as she was told, but the other one wrote down everything she had seen.

When you write it down, they cannot pretend it never happened.

CHAPTER ONE

They were walking home through the River Quarter in Amsterdam on the day before everything changed. The sisters were three years apart, and at fourteen and nearly eleven they were opposites in practically every way. Margot, the older girl, was beautiful, although she didn't seem to know it. The younger girl, Anne, had always been envious of her sister, for Anne might be considered ordinary, if you didn't know her. She had light brown eyes and dark hair, and she was always curious, making people laugh and talking nonstop as she entertained her friends in class, even during lessons. All the same, some people found her willful and headstrong. Most people didn't have any idea of who she was deep inside.

The sisters sometimes met after their classes to go home

together. Margot would make a detour to pick up her sister, then walk her bicycle. It was only ten minutes' time if they were quick about it, which they rarely were, for the weather was glorious, and today they lingered longer than usual. The world seemed perfect on this day, with bright sunlight falling through the branches of the trees. Why should they rush home to the chores that awaited them? They were young girls, in love with life and with all the possibilities of a wonderful future. It was May, their favorite time of the year, the season when the birds returned to nest in the trees along the river and the canals. Only the magpies stayed all year round and managed to survive the ice-cold winters, but now the skies were filled with migrating birds returning from Spain and Morocco.

"Let's go to Oase," Anne suggested. It was their favorite ice cream shop, and if they could, they would have stopped there every day.

"You know we can't," Margot answered, always the voice of reason.

"Can't or won't?" Anne grinned. *Let's break the rules*, she often urged her older sister. *Let's take a chance.* "We're already going to be late," Anne said cheerfully. "We might as well stop."

They had to pass the ice cream shop on their way from the school anyway. Going home meant starting their homework and setting the table and listening to their mother's questions and judgments about how they'd spent their day. Anne loved walking along the streets of their busy neighborhood to the Merwedeplein, the square where they lived, not far from the Amstel River. The neighborhood was filled with bicycles and cars, and the sisters always looked for the flower man, whose cart was pulled by a huge dog.

"Let's bring him home," Anne said when they spied the enormous white dog, who steadfastly towed the cart loaded down with tulips from the flower fields out in the countryside.

Margot laughed. "He'd take up our whole house."

"Good," Anne responded. "He'd make things interesting."

"And what do you think our mother's reaction would be? If he sat on a chair, he'd be tossed out the door."

The girls laughed at the idea of the gigantic dog being bossed around by their mother. Edith Frank insisted their house be kept neat and clean at all times, and dog hair and muddy pawprints would never be allowed. Their apartment was in a new building in a comfortable neighborhood with many Jewish residents who had fled from the Nazi regime in Germany. There were dozens of new apartment buildings in the neighborhood, including the tallest residential building in Amsterdam, called the Skyscraper, one with so many stories that little children living nearby said the top floor led into heaven. People claimed it was possible to see every star up above if you lived in the highest apartments. In the evenings, when the Frank sisters sat on the steps outside their apartment, they could see lights flickering in rooms that seemed to float above the tallest trees.

"If we stop at Oase, maybe someone will treat us," Anne suggested, for although she had no money of her own, there were often boys who were willing to buy girls ice cream. Anne was young, too young for boys some might say, but she liked to flirt, and what was the harm in doing so?

"We shouldn't take gifts from strangers," Margot instructed her little sister. She didn't know where Anne got her nerve, and there were times when she wished that she, herself, were a bit braver. She couldn't remember ever breaking a rule.

"Ice cream is not a gift," Anne insisted. "It's a necessity. And there's nothing wrong with friendship."

"Anne." Even Margot, easygoing as she was, could get annoyed by her sister's badgering. "Not today."

"Fine," Anne said, walking on ahead of Margot. They weren't friends, only relations, and Anne was certain she would have never chosen Margot as a friend; they had so very little in common.

"Don't bother trying to catch me," Anne called over her shoulder as she took off running. "Someday you'll wish you'd listened to me and had more fun."

★ ★ ★

Margot did her best to watch over her sister, but Anne had a mind of her own. She was perceptive and already interested in topics she wasn't supposed to know about at her age. The more she knew, the more puzzled she was by the workings of the world around her. Why were men allowed more freedom than women? Why did people fall in love? How did it happen, and when would it happen to her? Why had their family left their home in Germany? Why was there so much hatred in the world?

Margot was an excellent student, diligent and kind-hearted and athletic, and a valued member of the rowing team. She was enrolled in a high school that included students of all religions, with only five Jewish girls registered in a class of thirty or more. Anne, whose full name was Annelies Marie Frank, went to a Montessori school on Niersstraat, a wonderful place where students were allowed to write and paint as they saw fit, with classes based on a method that encouraged children to express themselves. The girls' parents knew their younger daughter needed the freedom to be herself; she couldn't sit still for very long and only paid attention to the subjects she liked, and she likely wouldn't have done well in the classes Margot attended. Anne's school felt like an enchanted place for those who had wild imaginations. There was a huge chestnut tree in the courtyard, and some people believed if you touched the bark of the tree your wish would be granted, but only if you closed your eyes, and only if you really believed. Anne was a believer, one who loved fairy tales and myths. She was certain girls could forge paths for themselves, no matter how dark and deep the forests might be.

I wish to be whoever I want to be, Anne whispered when she held the palm of her hand against the tree in the courtyard. *I wish to be myself.*

The sisters had lived in Amsterdam ever since Anne was four, when the family had fled Germany. The Netherlands still allowed Jews to enter when other countries, including the United States, had instituted quotas that kept out refugees, even though the conditions for Jews in Germany were worsening as the Nazi persecution grew more ruthless all the time. The Netherlands had been a refuge for Jews fleeing the Inquisitions in Spain and Portugal in the 15th and 16th centuries. It was a place rooted in equality, where much of the Jewish population was given full civil rights in 1796, allowed to live freely in a city that was both mysterious and practical, a world made of ice in the winter and of tulips in the spring. Back then, the city would flood with the rising tide; it had been built in the marshes, and people wore wooden shoes so they could walk through the mud as they tended their fields. Now Amsterdam was ringed by 165 canals, with countless bridges built across the waterways, for the swampland had been drained hundreds of years ago by wealthy merchants who had then built tall, elegant canal houses with fairy-tale gables. For those passing by, it was possible to imagine they had walked into a story, one in which good people were rewarded and those who were evil were locked up in the towers, the keys thrown away, tossed into the dark waters of the canals.

Anne liked to stop and gaze into the canals. She sometimes thought she could see what other people could not. There, in the still water, she imagined she saw pieces of the city's past. Bricks from houses that had fallen down, a necklace lost by a noblewoman, a silver fish that had been swimming in the canals for a hundred years.

"You're a dreamer," Margot always told her sister, for all Margot saw when she gazed at the canals was the dirty water and ducks paddling by. She saw boats making their deliveries and an occasional elegant white swan, too proud and vain to look back at her.

When Margot made such comments, Anne knew that even if you were sisters you could see the world in completely different ways. The *here and now* and the *what could be*. How dull to have no imagination, to see only what was right there in front of you. She thought of the fairy tale "Snow-White and Rose-Red," a story in which two sisters were different in every way, just as she and Margot were different. Anne sometimes thought her favorite words were *Once upon a time*, even though her mother always told her to wake up and pay more attention to her schoolwork and her chores and not always be reading one of her books. But the girls' father, Otto Frank, whom they called Pim, was a great reader, and what was so wrong with that? He was the one who understood Anne, even when her mother didn't.

Dreams are the beginning, he always told Anne. *They're the stories we tell ourselves.*

At the Montessori school, Anne's best friend was Hannah Goslar, called Hanneli or sometimes Hanne. Both girls had spent their earliest years in Germany, and they often whispered to each other in a language not many in their class understood. The two friends spent huge amounts of time together, for Hanneli also lived nearby in the River Quarter. Soon, they included another girl in their friendship, Susanne, who was called Sanne. Anne and Hanne and Sanne. They thought it was fate that they would be best friends with rhyming names, and they would never stop being friends— they had already decided that. They talked for hours about the future that awaited them and all they would do.

"We'll go to America," Anne said, for that was her dream, a story she told herself every night. *Once upon a time, we lived in Amsterdam, until we left and went across the sea.*

"And we'll live in the same house," Hanneli added.

"But who will pay for it?" Sanne was a realist who always wanted to know details.

"Whoever is in love with us," Hanneli suggested.

"No." Anne shook her head. "I'll pay for it," she told them. "I'll be famous by then."

They all grinned, for if Anne believed it, so did they. She always took charge, and her closest friends understood why. Anne had always thought she would be someone special. But whenever her friends left for their own homes, the truth was Anne felt far too alone. She felt as if anything could happen.

Maybe she wasn't special, maybe she would find herself alone in the darkness without anyone who understood her. Margot was who she appeared to be, sunny and bright and well-mannered, but Anne kept her truest self hidden, even from her closest friends. She was the cheerful girl who was always such fun, but she was smarter than anyone imagined, which was something she kept to herself. Let people think she was nothing beyond the person she showed on the outside, the dramatic girl who liked to act in plays, the chatterbox who often found herself in trouble at school. She was always reading and thinking, but she gazed out the window at the clouds when she should have been listening to her teachers and her parents. Anne's mother was often disapproving when Anne talked too much or acted as if she knew the answers to most questions, even though Edith was a big talker as well. But the girls' beloved grandmother Rosa Holländer, whom they called Oma, understood Anne.

If you want to know who she is, Oma had told Anne's mother, *look more deeply. Look inside.*

✳ ✳ ✳

The girls' grandmother spent nights sleeping in what had been the dining room but had been set up with a bed for Oma, a necessity now that the extra bedroom on the top floor was occupied by a boarder who helped pay the rent. Oma had been frail ever since she'd arrived from Germany a little over a year ago. She had lost everything, her home, her belongings, even the roses that grew in her garden; all of it had been taken by the government. In 1933, Adolf Hitler and his Nazi Party rose to power in the wake of Germany's loss in World War I, often called the Great War. Otto and Edith had sensed that conditions for Jews would grow worse under Hitler's regime. Soon, there were race laws in Germany, and Jews were no longer considered citizens, even if they had lived there all their lives, even if they had fought in the Great War to protect their country, even if they were doctors or teachers or famous writers. By 1940, German Jews were no longer allowed into parks or public schools or markets. Hate had become legal; it was everywhere.

First, Otto Frank came to the Netherlands in 1933, then Edith and Margot and Anne followed in 1934. The family had left long before the mayhem of November 9 and 10 in 1938, later known as Kristallnacht, the Night of Broken Glass, because the streets in Germany and Austria were littered with shards of broken glass after the Nazis' most violent public attack on the Jews. Bands of storm troopers and Hitler Youth ran wild, out for blood, beating and murdering Jews. Thousands of Jewish-owned shops and houses were destroyed, fourteen hundred synagogues were burned to the ground, and Jews were dragged from their homes simply because they were Jewish; murdered men were left on the street, women and children wept, and their cries echoed far into the countryside.

More than thirty thousand Jewish men were rounded up on Kristallnacht, then arrested and taken to concentration camps; even Anne's uncle Walter was arrested, though later released. People fled as if they were birds, for soon more concentration camps were built, and any Jew who didn't flee would be trapped in a cage for which there was no key. They were called labor camps, and it was said that those brought there to work would return home when their work was completed, but in time, the Jews in Germany came to realize those who were taken would never come back.

Anyone who didn't fly away soon discovered it was too

late. The sky was wide, but the world they inhabited was small, and before you knew it there was nowhere to escape to, and even the sky was crisscrossed by nets. Countries closed their borders, refusing to let Jewish refugees enter; boatloads of people were turned away from the shores of free countries and many had no chance to survive. Anne's family was thankful to have come to the Netherlands, a neutral country that had avoided taking sides in international issues. They would be safe here, the girls' father was sure of it, which was why Edith Frank's mother, Oma, had come to live with them in March 1939 as well.

They were settled in Amsterdam, and yet Oma dreamed of broken glass; she heard it shattering in her sleep, and sometimes she spent the night in a chair by the window so that she might keep watch, even though they were no longer in Germany. Oma heard something breaking apart. She heard the future that might await them.

One night Anne spied her grandmother peering out the window in the middle of the night, and she came to sit at Oma's feet.

"I thought I heard a riot outside," Oma said in a quiet voice.

Anne had heard about Kristallnacht, and she dreamed about it sometimes. In her dreams she saw people running down a dark street. There were men who were dragged underground, and women who turned into birds in order to fly away. Families who had been sitting in their own homes had been pulled into the street. People who had huddled in courtyards and office buildings were arrested and thrown onto a ground of glass. Oma had warned her that the worst things happened when you least expected them, they came the way a hard rain fell, when you had your eyes closed, when you were too busy thinking about other things. On an ordinary day, when the weather seemed fine, that's when it happened, that's when the whole world changed.

"Good people cannot understand evil. They don't even recognize it," Oma told her granddaughter. "That's what happened in Germany."

There had been small riots in Amsterdam, even close to their home, but that knowledge had been kept from Anne and her sister.

"Everything is fine here," Anne reassured her grandmother. "Maybe you heard the rabbits."

It was the time of year when the rabbits burrowed underneath the hedges during the day, but were often out at night when the grassy square was deserted.

Oma shook her head. "That's not what I heard."

Anne's eyes were bright. She understood things people would have assumed she was too young to notice. She knew that her grandmother was afraid that what was happening in Germany could also happen here. "You heard the past," Anne said.

Her grandmother leaned down and stroked Anne's hair. She had always had a special fondness for her younger granddaughter. Although some people felt Anne was too full of herself, Oma knew she was deeply sensitive, possessing a huge compassionate heart that was easily wounded, not that Anne showed her hurt to anyone, especially not to her mother, whom she often felt she could never please. Sometimes, when Anne was in her mother's presence, she would retreat into a world of her own. "Wake up," Edith would say then. "We're not here to dream."

I *am*, Anne would whisper under her breath. *I can dream whatever I want to.*

It was true Anne often forgot her chores, and everyday life didn't always interest her. Her imagination ran wild as she read novels in the fading light in the bedroom that she shared with Margot, so engrossed that the rest of the world slipped away. Her mother would knock on the door late at night, calling for Anne to turn out the light. But even after she'd done as she was told, Anne often couldn't sleep; she would look out her window to gaze at the stars, which seemed so close she sometimes felt as if she could reach out and touch them.

On this night, when she'd heard her grandmother in the parlor, she knew what it was like to feel alone, even when your house was filled with people. She knew how alone you could feel when everyone else was asleep, when you felt haunted by your own dreams.

"Dream of rabbits," she advised her grandmother that night.

"I'd rather dream about you," Oma told her. She agreed to go back to bed if Anne did the same.

"Let's dream about the future," Anne suggested.

"Fine," her Oma agreed. She felt better just talking to

Anne. How lucky she was to have a granddaughter who had hope. "Let's do that."

"We'll be in California," Anne said. "In a big house by the sea."

"Will we?" Oma laughed, delighted.

"I'm bringing you with me," Anne assured her grandmother.

"I'm ready," Oma said, kissing Anne good night. She could not love her granddaughter more.

When Anne went back to her room, Margot was dreaming, her breath soft and foggy, her face turned to the wall. Anne crept beneath her own blanket and closed her eyes. It was late, past midnight, but that didn't mean she was sleeping, and it didn't mean that out in the dining room Oma was either.

* * *

Anne loved to go out onto the flat roof when her friends came to visit. They had privacy there, and it seemed as if they could be anywhere in the world as they set up lawn chairs and sprawled out comfortably to read on a sunny afternoon.

"Maybe you should write a book about us," Hanneli suggested to Anne.

"Maybe," Anne said. She didn't want to make any promises. For now she was most interested in the tales her father told her, ones in which girls often saved their families and themselves.

All you needed to believe in yourself was to know that someone loved you, the real you, the you deep inside. Although Anne felt as if no one truly knew her, she knew that she was loved. She had her Oma, but she was also her father's favorite. She was sure of it, even if he never said so and did his best not to show it. They were two peas in a pod. Pim laughed at Anne's jokes and appreciated the fact that she yearned for more from life. He was calm and logical, but he was passionate as well, especially when it came to literature. He was a voracious reader and was proud that Anne was as well, even if that meant staying up late and breaking the rules. Pim influenced her greatly, especially when it came to reading, which he always said was never a waste of time.

Pim's father had risen to become a wealthy banker in Germany before Jews were blamed for the financial failures in that country following its defeat in World War I. All they had once possessed had been lost in the global turmoil, and they were left with nothing. The Franks had never been a religious family and had considered themselves Germans, but soon enough, like all other Jews, they were seen as outsiders. When they'd had to flee, Pim initially set up a jam and spice business in Amsterdam, through a German company, renting office space and hiring a partner, Johannes Kleiman, and an employee, Victor Kugler. He also brought in a young Austrian woman named Miep Santrouschitz, who had become his faithful assistant and was now considered a member of the family. A young secretary of eighteen named Elisabeth Voskuyl, called Bep, was hired, and she was devoted to the company as well.

Pim inspired loyalty in others and he was loyal in return. He was an honorable, hard-working man and he had given up his own dreams for the sake of his family. When he was young, he had worked in New York with his friend Nathan Straus Jr., whose family owned the famous Macy's department store in Herald Square in Manhattan. They had attended the University of Heidelberg together for a summer, and Pim had been best friends with Nathan, whom he called

Charley. Pim might have stayed in New York, for he loved that wild, busy city, but then his father passed away and he returned to be with his family and help them financially.

Nathan Straus Jr. was a wealthy, important man with strong ties to the US government. He'd been a member of the New York State Senate and had been appointed head of the United States Housing Authority by President Franklin D. Roosevelt. Straus was a friend of the first lady, Eleanor Roosevelt, who was a great believer in social justice, and who, from the beginning of the Nazi regime, had asked for aid for Jewish refugees. As far back as 1939, Eleanor Roosevelt had tried to persuade the government to pass a bill that would have allowed twenty thousand German Jewish refugee children to enter the States, but the bill was ignored and never voted on, and the children had not been allowed into the country. Later, most were taken to death camps and murdered. In the Nazi regime, age meant nothing, humanity meant nothing, love meant nothing.

If Otto Frank had remained in New York, if he hadn't been afraid of disappointing his mother and had instead done as he pleased, he might have had an entirely different life from the one he was living in Amsterdam. He thought about that some-times. He thought about it more and more all the time. He might have been in Manhattan right now, and if he'd had daughters, they would have walked down Fifth Avenue every Sunday, looking in store windows, going to the movies, run-ning through Central Park. He knew what happened when you did as you were told; you often lost the best part of your-self. People said that his daughter Anne should behave, she shouldn't talk so much and have such big dreams or be so certain of what she wanted, but Pim didn't always agree. Anne was special, that was all there was to it. She was not like everyone else, for better or for worse, with good qualities along with qualities that annoyed people, but most certainly with dreams that were hers alone.

Just don't fly away, Pim often teased Anne when she was daydreaming, and she would grin because that was exactly what she planned to do someday.

✳ ✳ ✳

On the beautiful May day when the sisters met and walked home from school, that day before everything changed, Anne gazed up at the magpies in the branches of the plane trees. The birds had gone through the cold Amsterdam winter, nesting in the tallest branches of the trees. The magpies were looking down at her with their jewel-like eyes, and although they were usually loud, they were silent on this May day. Magpies were members of the crow family, so clever and curious that some people said they were thieves. They took clothes from the laundry lines, rings from people's fingers, flowers from fenced gardens, grapes and pears from carts being pulled by horses. Perhaps this was why Anne admired them so. Magpies took what they wanted and did as they pleased. They went wherever they wished and they didn't flee as the other birds did when winter came. They stayed where they were, even when there was ice and snow; nothing could chase them away from Amsterdam.

Anne waved at the birds and whistled a tune. "Hello," she called out. "Can you teach me to fly?"

"Do you think they understand you?" Margot asked with a grin. She didn't know where Anne got her ideas—from books, she imagined, from the stories she overheard Pim telling her, magical tales in which anything could happen.

"Of course they do," Anne replied. She'd read that magpies recognized faces and could tell people apart. There was one that often followed her home from school, and she sometimes thought he waited for her until classes were over and she ran out to the street. She pointed at him now. "That one knows me."

"Anne, that's very unlikely," Margot said gently, as if she were speaking to someone who didn't understand a thing about the world. "These things don't happen."

Sometimes, Anne felt sorry for her sister. She wondered what it was like to be so good and unquestioning and how it felt to believe everything you were told and never imagine anything brand new. Margot didn't even notice that most of the boys who passed stared at her, but Anne did, and she understood why: Margot was a natural beauty and boys were instantly drawn to her. They usually ignored Anne, but recently she realized that whenever she started to talk they gathered around, charmed and wanting to hear what she had to say, which was quite a lot. When that happened, Anne knew she was worth talking to, even if she wasn't yet eleven, even if she wasn't as pretty as Margot. Once she started talking, the light inside her began to shine and that was when other girls didn't seem the least bit interesting. It was a gift, her Oma had told her, a kind of magic all her own. Being pretty wasn't everything, but feeling that you were worth something was.

The sisters went out of their way so they could pass by the Blankevoort Bookstore, one of their favorite places, just around the corner from home.

"We have to stop here," Anne said. "Just for a few minutes!"

"Not here either." Margot laughed. "We're late!"

Still, they took a moment to stare inside at the shelves of books. Anne wished that she lived in a bookshop and could read all night long. In every bookshop in Amsterdam there seemed to be a black cat and over nearly every door there was a bell that rang when you walked inside. Anne and Pim had visited shops looking for old volumes. They especially loved investigating the bookstalls set up outside at the book market, where books were stuffed onto rickety shelves in no particular order, so that fairy tales were mixed in with poetry, history and novels were side by side, and every book was a surprise.

Whenever they were out together, Pim told Anne her

favorite stories, old German fairy tales, along with Greek and Roman mythology, a subject he had studied while at university in Heidelberg. Sometimes, he told tales he'd made up, which Anne liked best of all. Her favorite stories were about girls who were locked away but who discovered a way to free themselves, girls who leaped from tall towers, who climbed down thorny vines and ran through the mossy woods to find safety among the trees.

"We could be just a little late," Anne suggested to her sister as they walked on. She was one of those girls, like the ones in her stories, who yearned for freedom. How she would love to prowl around inside the bookshop without having to keep time on the clock, then stop at a café to have a lemonade and a roll topped with cream cheese and chocolate. What difference would ten minutes make? Even half an hour? It wouldn't matter to anyone, but it would open the world for her if she could have a life in which she could do as she pleased.

"Not today," Margot insisted. When Anne sighed, Margot added, "It's so much easier when you do as you're told."

"I'm sure it is. For you."

Anne made a face and they both laughed. That was the

thing about being someone's sister. You could hate her and love her at the very same time. You could tell her things you wouldn't tell anyone else or tell her nothing at all. You could have a fight and say horrible things, and then forget all about it. You could outrun her when she least expected you to do so, just take off and know she would follow.

They raced past the billowy trees, a mad dash so they wouldn't be too late to help fix dinner. As the girls neared home, Margot saw their building in the distance, beyond the green park bordered by hedges and flower beds. Unlike her sister, Anne saw not only what was, but what might be. She was beside Margot as they turned the corner, but she already had one foot in the future, ready to leap into the life she wanted, one that was far away from here. She was a magpie, she was an escape artist, and she didn't intend to stay put and live the life everyone else thought she should. All girls had dreams, and Anne certainly had hers, which she kept secret not only from Margot, but from her closest friends as well. She might look ordinary, she might seem like any other girl on the street, but she knew she was something more.

She was just waiting to find out what that was.

CHAPTER TWO

In fairy tales there were two parts of every story, the inside and the outside. The outside was green and bright, just as it was now when they walked home from school, trying not to be late on the day before something unthinkable was about to happen, something they would have never expected as they talked about ice cream and books. The inside of the story was the stone that no one could see, hidden in the center, like the pit of a fruit, one so sharp it could cut you if you reached for it. It was tomorrow, and the day after that, and the years that would soon come. Anne had faith in the future. She often imagined that she would someday go to California. She would ride down the Pacific Coast Highway and live in Hollywood and become an actress. But on this day when they were late, she thought she could see a shadow following them. Standing in the dappled sunlight that spread through the leaves of the trees like lace, Anne felt a sudden chill. She looked up past the Skyscraper, where all the windows reflected the bright sky, and she wondered if the weather would change, even though winter had passed and it was now the most beautiful month of the year.

There outside her own home, she had caught a glimpse of the inside of the story, the one their parents didn't want them to know, the reason fairy tales warn children to beware at every turn. You cannot know when evil will appear. That was the inside of the story, waiting to open like a dark flower. She could only see its shadow from the corner of her eye, a large black moth. She spied it only for an instant, but it was long enough for Anne to tug on her sister's hand and say *Hurry*, and then they ran so fast it was almost as if they were flying.

The family lived at number 37 Merwedeplein, and the sisters often raced up the stoop two steps at a time to see who could get to the door first and run inside. But this time they paused at the threshold. They could hear raised voices inside. Their apartment had a sign that asked visitors to ring three times (3 X BELLEN), but the girls often barked three times instead, reading the word *bellen* for its German meaning, *bark*. Now, however, Margot gripped Anne's arm to keep her from entering.

"Let's give them a minute," Margot whispered. Their parents had had more to disagree about since coming to the Netherlands, and Margot's eyes shone with empathy. She wanted to believe all would be well. "Husbands and wives argue. It doesn't mean anything's wrong," Margot told Anne when she saw the worried look on her sister's face.

This time their parents were quarreling about Anne, whose teachers had complained about her. *Starry-eyed. Dreamer. Doesn't pay attention. Talks when she should be quiet. Talks all the time.* Anne had been chattering to her friends when she should have been paying attention to her lessons. Even though her teacher didn't appreciate Anne doing as she pleased, she usually also praised her for being bright and independent.

"She's special," Anne heard her father say as he argued with their mother, which made her love him all the more.

Pim was such an elegant, generous man, handsome and educated, but also kindhearted. He saw his younger daughter for who she was, the girl who was always questioning, who had so much to say, the one who wished she could fly away and see the whole world.

"Why does she always need to be special?" Anne's mother responded grimly, a remark that made Anne's cheeks flush with shame. "Let her be like everyone else and get her work done properly and not have her head in the clouds. If she thinks she's special, she'll be disappointed."

Anne remembered once overhearing her father's mother, Omi, discussing with an aunt how Anne's parents' marriage was more of a business agreement than a love story. "Duty and family are not enough. You should never marry someone you don't love." Anne had gone into the garden to crouch beneath the lilac hedge. There were three blue duck eggs hidden there, one for the present, one for the past, and one for the future. The mother duck had disappeared, and Anne wondered if the eggs would even hatch, and maybe that was why she'd begun crying. It was the first time she had realized that children weren't told the truth.

Ever since that time, Anne had seen her parents differently, as a team, two people who had come to an agreement, and even if they weren't always happy, they would stay together for the sake of the family, and the children, and the household. This was not the sort of marriage Anne wanted when she grew up. She wanted a true love, she wanted to be special, and she wished that her mother wanted that for her too.

When the sisters entered the apartment, their parents stopped arguing immediately. Margot and Anne slipped off their jackets, then washed their hands and quickly began to set the table. "Here at last," their mother said, noting their lateness before turning to the stove.

Anne swallowed the words that still bloomed inside her but went unsaid. *Can't you be nicer to him? Can't you love me for who I am? If you ever lost me, would you cry until the world was flooded and the fields were turned to ice? Would you follow me to the ends of the earth no matter the cost?*

Their grandmother was already at the table, and Oma reached for Anne and hugged her fiercely, as if she would protect her from all the troubles of the world. "You will always be special to me," Oma said.

There were carrots cooking, and noodles cooling in a colander in the sink. Oma always managed to make a delicious meal, no matter the ingredients. Tonight they would have a simple dish for dinner called kugel, which was a favorite, but best of all, their father had brought home a rare delight for after their meal, bolus, Dutch sweet rolls flavored with cinnamon and filled with raisins and candied citrus peel, a recipe that had arrived with the Spanish Jews fleeing the Inquisition.

As Anne went to fetch glasses for their lemonade, she stopped in the parlor and gazed out the window. She spied the magpie in the trees. He had followed her home, she was sure of it. Magpies could tell one person from another and she could now tell one magpie from another. This one was hers. She waved to the bird, and he tilted his head. He knew her, perhaps better than her own family did. She would leave out breadcrumbs for him and perhaps he would build a nest nearby. The future was right there in front of them and maybe she could fly away as the birds did and have the life that she wanted. All she had to do was wait to grow up, and then she could do whatever she pleased.

"How is my beautiful girl?" her Oma asked when dinner was over. They ate at the dining table that had been pushed away from her bed. Even though Oma had lost everything when she left Germany, she hadn't lost her family and that was all that mattered, she always said.

"I wish I could act in a play," Anne told her grandmother, a smile breaking across her face. Something inside of her lit up when she talked to someone who understood her. She liked to talk about herself, and she knew she was too much for some people, those who wanted her to behave and be a quiet, sweet girl, not one who had ambition. She wanted to play the part of Esther, the biblical queen who had saved her people. When she closed her eyes, Anne could see herself in an ancient land where olive trees grew. She could see herself walking down to the banks of the Euphrates River, where the water was as blue as the sky.

"I assume you'll be the star," Oma said.

"Of course." Anne grinned. She knew that some of the girls at school thought she was too full of herself and too honest in her remarks, but her grandmother understood her. They grinned at each other, but only for a moment, for Edith had joined them, and she liked conversation to be serious, with everyone reporting on the events of their day.

"What happened at school?" she asked now.

"It was like any other day," Anne said. She knew that any answer she gave would displease her mother. Edith wouldn't have been interested in Anne's play anyway. *Your schoolwork is what matters most*, she always said, even though she could tell that Anne wasn't listening to the rules her mother set out, and it was likely she never would. She was too busy dreaming to hear a word Edith said.

* * *

Before going to sleep, Margot helped Anne write to her pen pal, Juanita, in America. Juanita was the younger sister of Margot's pen pal. Anne's uncles had settled in Massachusetts, and Anne wished her family had gone there as well, but by the time her father had applied for visas to get them to the States, they were on the waiting list. They were hoping for good news, and Pim always said they would be in America before too long.

Anne wrote to her pen pal, pouring out her heart to a stranger she had never met, for the girls she knew often didn't understand her, not even Sanne and Hanneli. *Hoping to hear from you*, Anne signed off. She would mail the letter later in the week, but she would never hear back.

When it was quite late, and the paper and ink had been put away, Anne's mother came to say good night. She was strict with Anne, and she knew she could seem harsh. She was protective, but her words of advice often came off as if she was being critical of Anne. She intended to explain herself to her daughter. *I'm afraid if you want too much you will be disappointed in life* was what she wanted to say, but before she could, Anne sat up to face her mother. She was surprisingly matter-of-fact and if she was wounded by her mother's words, she didn't show it. She had made a vow to herself to never reveal when she was injured by anyone's opinion of her. She would be herself no matter what, just as her Oma had told her she should.

"You don't have to worry about me," Anne told her mother. If her mother could only care about a daughter who was perfect, she would likely only care about Margot. "Oma worries about me enough," Anne said. "So you don't have to."

"I just want you to be happy," Edith told her daughter.

Edith Frank didn't often speak so tenderly. She had always thought it was best to have a tough skin and not show your emotions. That was the way to protect yourself from being hurt. "Are you happy?" Edith whispered to Anne.

Edith was speaking in German, but she didn't realize it. It was the language she had used when Anne was a baby, when she had sung to Anne each night. There was an old folktale that said the demon Lilith came to steal babies, and so Edith tied a red string around Anne's ankle, to make certain she wasn't spirited away. She could not have loved her daughters more, so much so that she was afraid to show it for fear she would be tempting fate.

Anne kept her face to the wall. She usually responded right away, but now it took a while before she could answer. She wasn't happy being almost eleven, but she would be when she was older. She was sure of it.

"I will be," she answered in a soft voice. "I'll be so happy you won't believe it."

By now there was no one to hear her, for Edith had already gone out into the hall and she didn't hear what Anne had to say. It seemed rude and unfeeling to Anne that her mother hadn't even waited for her answer, but Edith simply hadn't wanted Anne to see there were tears in her eyes. She made a point of never crying in front of her daughters when she feared what the future might be. Tears wouldn't get you anywhere in this world. The truth was she did think Anne was special, and she knew what grief that could bring. It was best to be ordinary and go unnoticed. If you did so, if you were quiet and cautious, then hopefully you would manage to get through the trials of this life. Edith prayed that bad fortune would not come anywhere near them, that it would not sit on the roof or reach in through the window or knock on the door. She might not show her feelings as a mother, but she had them all the same. She felt too much, and if she ever lost one of her daughters she would cry until the world was flooded. She would weep until the fields turned to ice. She would travel underground if need be, to the underworld, that dark place from which few managed to return.

The Frank sisters dreamed in German, slipping into the language of their earliest memories, a time when they hid beneath the lilac trees at their other grandmother's house. That grandmother was their father's mother, Alice Frank-Stern, and they called her Omi to distinguish her from their dear Oma who lived with them now. Their grandmothers were as different as night is from day. Oma was warm and endearing, while Omi was elegant and demanding. Family was everything, their mother often said. They will be there for you when everyone else disappears.

Omi had eluded the Nazis by leaving Germany for Basel, Switzerland, and now the sisters barely remembered her house, not even whether or not there had been a garden. Had there really been wisteria or had they imagined the purple blooms that wrapped around the porch, with petals that covered the ground when the wind blew them down? Were the lilacs really so tall that when Anne and Margot hid behind the bushes no one could find them or had they simply been so small back then? Their early childhood was another world to them now, a lost world.

Good people often could not understand why the oldest stories were filled with demons and dangerous beasts. They had no idea that when evil appears, you cannot fight it with arrows or stones. It is invisible and it is everywhere. The first sign is the scent of something burning, as if a fire had been set and the air was filling with black acrid smoke. It's best to run into the woods when this happens, even if there are wolves sleeping beneath the trees. You know what a wolf is the minute you see it, but an evil person can be hidden from sight. He's often in disguise. He can look like your neighbor, or a woman in a shop where you buy groceries, or like the person you thought was your friend.

Anne knew things she wasn't supposed to know, because she had overheard her parents talking when they thought she was fast asleep. She slipped from her room into the corridor, then sat on the steps in the hallway where she wouldn't be noticed.

"What if we chose wrong?" Anne heard her mother say. "What if we should have gone elsewhere?"

"The Netherlands was, is, and always will be a free nation," Otto replied. "You have to believe in some things. You have to put your faith in what is good."

The Franks had come here because it was one of the most tolerant countries in Europe with a long history of freedom and acceptance, having been neutral during the Great War. "We'll be safe there," Otto Frank had told his family and friends, and everyone had agreed. Why should they have any doubts?

Amsterdam had seemed an obvious place to run to because of its open-door policy for refugees who could afford the legal paperwork, but all foreigners were requested to register with the government. The Franks were outsiders again, and it was just the beginning, only they didn't know it. Hatred arises so quickly that one drop is all it takes before it spreads like ink on a page. Still, the girls' father was convinced the rising tide of prejudice against the Jews was a temporary evil stirred up by a few bad people. Evil could disappear, like smoke, like ashes. Most people were good at heart, he was sure of it, and this dark night was a storm that would pass as all storms did.

"We will see it through," Pim told his wife, "until we come to the other side."

But Anne wondered if it was possible for a girl to be so worried that even when she was in her own bed she walked through the woods all alone. She listened for wolves when the moon rose, even though they lived in the city of canals, in a country where a wild wolf had not been seen for nearly fifty years. At night, Anne dreamed of goblins, and when she awoke in the morning, she wondered what they would find waiting for them.

✳ ✳ ✳

"There are wars," Pim had told Anne and Margot to comfort them the next day. "But there is also peace," he assured the girls. "That is what most people want. A world where their children are safe, where they can sleep through the night, where all people can walk down the street and not be arrested because of who they are. You will see," Pim vowed. "We'll be safe here."

And yet, when they sat down to dinner, Anne noticed that her father was still standing by the window after the meal had been set on the table, a distracted expression on his face while he gazed into the empty square, as if waiting for the darkness to come. In the dark, the empty streets glowed in the glare of the streetlights. Of the nearly fifty thousand Jews who had applied to move to the Netherlands, trying to escape the chaos in Germany, only twenty-five thousand had been allowed to enter, not as citizens but as refugees, lost souls without a country of their own. That was what the sisters were now, only they didn't know it yet. They were outsiders here in Amsterdam, and when some people are less than others, and only a select few have rights, anyone who doesn't belong can never be safe.

CHAPTER THREE

It happened at dawn, the thing they didn't expect, the day like no other. All at once it seemed as if a rain of stars had tumbled from the sky. It was three a.m., the hour when the birds were asleep, when the fish in the canals drowsed in the shallows. The racket sounded like hail, and then like stones being thrown. But when the sky lit up, it was because bombs were going off out in the countryside. There were no falling stars—only this, this burst of weapons that dropped from above.

The roar that at first appeared to be thunder was the sound of German bombers flying over Amsterdam on their way to bomb the airport. Anne and her sister looked at each other in the dim morning light, then hurried out of bed without saying a word. When they went into the parlor, their parents and Oma were there in their nightclothes, already listening to the radio. Pim had tuned in to their connection to the world that had not been struck down by the sudden madness outside. They had been overrun by enemy forces. Margot took her sister's hand and they stood with their backs against the wall.

It was a Friday morning, but the schools would remain closed and people would stay off the streets and stay home rather than go to work. Edith Frank did her best to act as if it were an ordinary day, and it seemed to be so to the sisters, although they were told they must stay inside. They dressed and did their chores, but then Anne happened to spy her mother and grandmother frantically looking through the pantry, making certain there was enough food to last for several weeks if need be. Anne stopped in her tracks to watch. They were in a panic, that much was clear, speaking in German, as if they had never escaped from their home country, for bad luck and misfortune seemed to have followed them here. The Netherlands was a neutral country that did not hold itself to be a part of any ongoing war. Germany had ignored that status and had attacked anyway.

Pim saw Anne in the corridor. He went to her and told her not to worry. "We're fine," Pim said. "We will be safe."

"How can you be sure?" Anne asked.

"The rest of the world will come to the aid of the Netherlands. It's illegal for the Germans to be here."

Anne nodded and leaned against her father. He had courage, and so should she. But there was the echo of air raids all day, and the sirens got inside a person's head and filled it with all sorts of terrible thoughts.

"Let's do our schoolwork," Margot suggested when she found Anne up on the third floor, looking through the glass into the sky. "It will give us something to do."

"Why should we bother?" Anne thought she saw something strange out on the roof. A huge black moth fluttering against the windowpanes. Then she blinked and it was gone.

"Of course we should! We'll be back in school next week."

"Maybe we won't ever go back to school." Anne didn't sound snippy or full of herself. She didn't sound in the least bit special. She sounded like a ten-year-old girl who was afraid of the sky, and of the black moth, and of the possibility that her beloved father might be mistaken.

Margot looped her arm around her sister. "Pim said we'll get through this, and we will."

* * *

But by evening, the announcers on the radio told people to keep their lights off so the German planes would have trouble navigating the city. People tried their best to leave Amsterdam, with hundreds waiting to flee. The Franks had no car, and no place to go, so they watched from the windows while the streets backed up with bicyclists and carts as neighbors did their best to escape, their belongings strapped to their backs. What they thought would never happen had happened overnight.

Anne remembered her father telling her that in ancient times salt was given as an offering at the Temple in Jerusalem, for it was thought to heal and purify, and it was a symbol of the eternal. She found the saltshaker in the cupboard and brought it into the bedroom, where she sprinkled salt onto the floor.

Margot shook her head as Anne went to each corner of their room. "This is nonsense, Anne. You know that, don't you?"

Anne could feel her throat burning. "You think everything I do is nonsense."

Margot came to wrap her arms around Anne. "I do not."

Anne melted into her sister. "You don't have to be nice to me," she told Margot. Anne was embarrassed to be acting like a baby, especially when they had never been that close. Why should they pretend to be now? They were nothing alike.

"I *want* to be nice to you," Margot said. "A sister is more than a friend."

Anne looked up at Margot, who had never appeared more beautiful. She could feel the familiar sting of her own jealousy. Sometimes she wished they could change places. "I would do anything for you," Margot said with a natural kindness that made Anne even more envious of her sweet nature. "And I'll always be your sister."

On this night, Anne cried and allowed Margot to stroke her hair. She hoped that she would always remember this moment when all she felt was love for her sister rather than resentment, when she didn't care if Margot was the perfect daughter, when it didn't matter that she was the self-centered one who wanted to fly away over the rooftops, past the canals, past the river and the plane trees, to a world where there was sunshine all year round, where the birds in the trees were the only sound she could hear.

* * *

On the day after the bombings, Pim was in the front room all day long, the radio turned on as announcers did their best to explain what had happened to the world they had once known. It had been a long, quiet day, and now the girls had been called into the kitchen to help set out dinner.

"I'll get the plates," Margot said.

"Silverware," Edith said, coming between them, giving her younger daughter a look for not seeing to her chores. "Someday you'll have your own table in your own kitchen; you should know how to set out a meal."

They would have the leftovers from the night before, the same noodles and cheese, so no food would be wasted. Anne held the tureen, even though it was burning her hands.

This was the night when she began to see what her parents didn't want her to see. They wanted to protect her, but she saw past the shadows. The moth, the salt, her father standing at the window, a voice on the radio, the birds all silent. Somewhere there were stars; surely they would be sprinkled through the night sky in California; there would be swirls of them, so many they would be a ladder into the heavens. Anne turned and saw her mother in the doorway. Edith looked like a stranger, wild-eyed with quiet fear. They had dinner in silence.

The streets were deserted once darkness fell, and on this night it felt as if they lived on the moon. They felt so far away, even from their neighbors next door. They might as well have been up in the trees, high above the earth. Oma brewed tea made from blue flowers that could only be found in the mountains in Switzerland. The blue tea would be the last gift they ever received from their Omi in Basel, but they didn't know that yet. The kitchen still smelled as it always had when Oma made her noodle pudding, especially when she sweetened the leftovers by adding the few pears that were still in the bin. It was May 11, the day after the unexpected had already happened. They listened to the radio, they heard what sounded like stars crashing to earth, and when night fell and the black moth appeared at the window, no one saw it, no one heard it tapping on the glass.

What We Lost

We could not sleep through the night after the bombs had fallen. Our family had scattered all over the world, but we did not fit into the quota of Jews allowed into America or England or Switzerland. We still thought it was impossible for the race laws in Germany to be put into effect here. We believed in what was fair.

We didn't understand that hatred changes everything and, in the morning, when we woke, we found we were afraid of the world outside.

It was far too quiet. It no longer belonged to us.

It was a place where anything could happen.

There were no longer ordinary days.

We stepped outside into a different world.

PART TWO

The Wolf
Amsterdam, May 1940–September 1940

You think of the forest with its dark and endless woods and you wish you were there right now, safe among the trees. When you hear a noise, you think your sister is following you, but she doesn't run that fast, she doesn't leap from a cliff or breathe so loudly, she doesn't try to catch you and take you down to the ground.

That's when you know it's best not to be here. They'll catch you if they can. If you hesitate, you will be lost. If you turn to look, you'll freeze in place. You hear them behind you right now. You hear them say your name.

That's when you begin to run.

CHAPTER FOUR

Three days after the bombs fell, the queen escaped from the country. She'd lost her power overnight and a British destroyer had taken her across the North Sea to England. Anne knew what happened when a queen disappeared in fairy tales. It was the moment when everything was lost, when cities crumbled, when the trees withered, when people no longer knew what to do.

The queen denounced Adolf Hitler as the archenemy of mankind and vowed she would return, but for now the Dutch were at the mercy of the Germans, who were stronger with a huge, well-trained army. The Dutch soldiers fought hard, but on May 15, two days after the queen left the country, when Rotterdam had been bombed and there was a threat to other Dutch cities, they surrendered. When the bombing stopped, when there was no longer the constant roar of noise that meant buildings were being destroyed and lives were being lost, there should have been a deep sense of relief. But the quiet meant the Germans had taken over. And because of this, the silence was terrifying. There were German soldiers in the streets of Amsterdam. It was as if a curtain had fallen and day had become night.

Lock the door, stay inside, don't trust anyone, don't talk too much, let's wait and see what will happen. Let's have hope.

The Franks had always imagined that if they ever needed to leave Amsterdam, they could go to stay with Pim's mother in Basel, but now Switzerland had all but closed its doors to immigrants. There was little hope for anyone attempting to enter Switzerland via the perilous climb through the mountains, and those refugees who managed to slip onto trains were turned back when they arrived at the border, even though it meant certain death to Jews who were forced to return to Germany. People ran into the forests; they slept in trees and drank from streams and many were shot down by soldiers.

Anne was upset that the Dutch had lost so quickly, but

Margot insisted there was nothing to worry about. She was an optimist, a believer in all that was good. "In six months we won't even be here," she declared. "We'll be in America."

Even though Pim's applications for visas to get them to America had all been destroyed in the bombing of Rotterdam, the sisters had always believed their father's opinions, and the fact that he still had a positive attitude was contagious. Still, once the Germans had arrived, Anne slept fitfully, despite Pim's insistence that in a few days life would settle down. The sisters often left their beds and went to peer out the window of the front room that overlooked the square. Nothing was out there, just their neighborhood, the same as always, a place filled with many Jewish families, where children played outside on summer nights, and parents stood on the street and chatted. Even though the Dutch had been defeated, the city looked the same. The same trees, the same sky, the bicycles in the streets, the rabbits in the grass. Perhaps it would remain as it had been before the bombing, which had mostly taken place outside of Amsterdam, and all they had to do was wait until life returned to normal. Their father must be correct in his hopeful assessment of what was to come, but sometimes it is hard to believe what you're told even for those who want to see the good in the world. Sometimes, Anne thought she saw the fluttering black moth tapping at the windows; she saw flowers that were fading for no reason even though it was the month of May, their petals turning brittle and gray. In the evenings, everyone stayed at home. Perhaps that was why there were more and more rabbits, more than they'd ever seen before. They ran through the square in the twilight as if the whole world belonged to them after curfew, as if they hadn't a worry in the world, unaware that where there are rabbits, there will soon be wolves.

"What do you think will happen now that the Germans are here?" Anne asked her grandmother one day when they were alone in Oma's bedroom, once the dining room. There was a china cabinet filled with dishes on one shelf and Oma's clothes folded on another. There was a bottle of perfume on the table beside her bed. She still sat up at nights looking out the window, and that worried Anne.

Oma seemed to have the ability to sense what the future

would be, not because she was a fortune teller, but because she had experienced the past. If you have been to a place once, you know it is possible to go there again. Time is a circle, and what happens in one country can begin in another. Terror can grow beyond borders, a forest of black trees with thorns on every branch. What happened in Germany had begun as a tiny seed of hatred, the smallest blister, a few evil men. How could Oma tell her beloved granddaughter what could happen when that seed bloomed? How could she reveal to her sweet child that evil was everywhere, in the hearts of your neighbors, and the postman, and your friends next door? Hatred was contagious, it spread from one household to the next, a slow infection of the spirit and the soul.

In Germany, before 1933, some Jews didn't see what was happening at first. The changes were nearly invisible before then, shadows you could only see from the corner of your eye. The Germans put on a play, a pantomime of what was to come, separation for the good of the nation. Then the curtain dropped, and people saw what was before them. There it was, the evil that had been there all along was revealed to one and all. The storm troopers with their Nazi armbands, the

Jews beaten and murdered, the children crying, the wind in the trees that sounded as if the whole world had been broken in two and nothing could put it back together again.

"No one knows what will happen," Oma told her darling Anne. "The future is a mystery."

Oma averted her eyes and made a sound in her throat that almost sounded as if she were choking on her own words. It was hard not to tell her granddaughter the truth, but she couldn't be sure of what would come to be. Why should she upset Anne when she might well be wrong about the future she feared was lurking close by, echoing what had happened to the Jews in Germany? Still, Oma shivered as she thought of the link between the past she had known to the future they were about to enter. How do you tell your granddaughter that life can be tragic for no reason? How do you say that to any decent person who wants to believe that life is fair?

"My parents say we'll be fine." Anne wasn't sure whether or not she believed them, but she knew that Oma would never lie to her; that was why she had come to speak to her grandmother. "Is what they say true?"

"The truth can be many things." Oma shrugged. Lately,

her hands had begun to shake and she no longer took up her embroidery. "We can never know the future."

"But what do *you* think?" Anne asked.

"I think you'll grow up to be a beautiful woman," Oma told her.

Anne laughed then. She couldn't help herself. It was so like Oma to give her a compliment, even in the midst of a serious discussion. "You only think I'm beautiful because I'm your granddaughter! Thank you, Oma, but I know I'm not, and frankly I don't care. I want more than that."

Oma was always intrigued by her younger granddaughter, who was unafraid to speak out. Yes, Anne could be opinionated, but she was brave as well, and she saw the world in her own way. How lovely that the way things looked wasn't what meant most to her. How deeply her granddaughter looked at the world.

"What is it that you want?" Oma asked, curious. It was almost as if they were both girls in this moment, peering into the future together, imagining what it might bring.

"I don't know yet," Anne admitted. She was just a girl who knew so little of the world. She was at the end of something and at the beginning of something. Still, it was just a matter of time before she knew exactly who she wished to be.

✳ ✳ ✳

That afternoon Edith watched her daughters, who were reading on the flat roof, lazing in the sun and stretching out on the old cloth-covered wooden lawn chairs. For a moment it seemed as if the world hadn't changed. Anne was reading a novel about a group of Dutch friends, and Margot had come out and pulled up a chair so that she could study history. Edith had a sinking feeling as she gazed at her girls. Everything had changed, and it would continue to do so, little by little, piece by piece. Oma had told Edith that Anne had come to her, worrying over what the German invasion would mean to them. Only a fool wouldn't be worried, and Anne was no fool.

Edith wondered if their destination had been the wrong choice. Perhaps they had made a terrible mistake coming to Amsterdam. She had begun to think they should have gone to Switzerland as Otto's mother had, or sent the girls to stay with Otto's cousins in England—even France might have been better. They had reasoned it out before making their decision, and Otto had thought it best for the family to stay together. It had made perfect sense at the time. How could they have known what was to be, for the Germans themselves hadn't decided to attack the Netherlands until this year. Edith tried to stop herself being caught up in her worst fears, but it did no good; she carried them with her, and was haunted by them. What would she do if her daughters were taken from her? She knew without having to consider: She would walk over thorns and through sticks and stones, go to the ends of the earth. She would make any trade, pay any price, give up her own life. Anything, everything, to keep them safe.

Anne turned to see the hard expression on her mother's face as Edith watched her. She thought it was likely she had done something to displease her mother and that was why Edith was staring. There were so many things she might have done that had disappointed her mother, placed the spoons where the forks should go on the table, not been a beauty like her sister, said something foolish, acted vain and full of herself, read a novel when she should have been seeing to her schoolwork.

"What's wrong?" Anne asked her mother.

"It's nothing," Edith insisted. If she told her daughters her fears, she would frighten them, so she was careful to stand up straight and not give anything away. They were children, really, two young girls sitting in the sun on the rooftop, which already felt like an unsafe place. People wondered if soon enough, Jews would not be allowed into their own gardens; if they wouldn't be able to enjoy the flowers they had grown or walk outside to see the moon.

Parents think their children don't hear when they whisper about all that is wrong; they think their daughters don't know when they hide in the kitchen to cry. Parents convince themselves they can stare at their children with a blank expression and their children won't know that something is amiss. Life had changed, but they insisted it would change back. This bad time was temporary, a season of hatred, and such seasons never lasted, they vanished as time went on and everything would be as it was.

Except that now, several black moths tapped at the window. Anne watched them through the glass and wondered where they had come from. There had only been one, and that one had seemed like a shadow that had arisen from her imagination, but now there were more all the time. Anne was fairly certain that one had slipped in through a window or flitted through an open door. She spied it in a corner, though it was invisible to most people's eyes. It was there when her father said sleep tight, when he sat down with his book in his favorite chair, when he called her his darling girl. She saw the worry in his face. She saw the look of alarm in her mother's eyes when Edith stood in the doorway to the roof watching her. Her parents were afraid, even in their own home. She knew that to be true, whether or not they said it aloud.

The future arrived the way a wolf walked through the woods, silent as it passed through the neighborhood, searching for ways to satisfy its hunger. What you don't hear you don't see, not unless you narrow your eyes and peer through the dark. You have to light a candle and gaze beyond the treetops. You have to be prepared to see what you hoped you would never see. German soldiers on street corners, walking along the canals, massing in groups near the Amstel River. They wore metal helmets and heavy boots. They studied everyone they came upon with a cool glance, wary, checking for what they considered to be Jewish features—dark hair, dark eyes, individuals they thought were shifty and racially inferior. In the neighborhood, everyone did their best to avoid the soldiers; they crossed the street so they wouldn't be asked any questions. People whispered that lists had already been drawn up by the Germans with the names of Dutch Jews to arrest, from the radicals to the wealthy to writers and teachers.

It was warm out and the trees in the parks were green. There were boats in the canals and so many bicycles on the streets you could hear their bells ringing on every corner. Many people were resigned to their situation. *Is life really so bad? We have dinner with our families, our children are safe at home. In time the Germans will leave, they will forget us and go on to another country; why would they bother with us, why would they stay?*

* * *

Anne and Margot returned to their schools, and both made certain to come home more quickly, as their mother had instructed. Sometimes they would find each other after school and stop at the Oase ice cream shop, where Jews often met, the students their age to socialize, the adults to discuss the political situation in discreet voices. Resistance groups were starting to form, meeting in secret, mapping out what they would do when the Germans took their next lethal step. Not *if*, not *maybe*, simply *when*. In time, the underground resistance would hide twenty-five thousand to thirty thousand Jews.

Anne's friends Sanne and Hanneli often came to visit. They were more sophisticated than many of the other girls their age, and this was especially true of Anne, who'd had a crush on a thirteen-year-old boy named Peter Schiff. She was a flirt and interested in boys, but she depended upon Hanneli and Sanne. When the three friends were together in the apartment, it was easy to forget the problems in the country, at least for an hour or two. They played Monopoly and read novels up on the roof on sunny afternoons when it felt like summer, when it felt the world was the way it used to be.

But when Anne's friends went home and the apartment

was quiet again, she had an empty feeling. When she was alone, she spent most of her time on the roof, the place where she always felt most comfortable. When she held a hand over her eyes, she could see so far. The buildings below looked like toys from the rooftop, small enough to hold in the palm of your hand. Small enough to break.

After dusk, everyone was ordered to put blackout screens over their windows for safety's sake. At dinner, the family sat at the table, listening to the radio. The queen sometimes spoke, doing her best to be encouraging about the future. But she was in England, and they were here. They listened to the BBC and the voices of broadcasters from across the sea as they waited for the rest of the world to wake up to what had happened.

When a free independent country is invaded and bombed by another country, it is an act not only of war, but of terror. Shouldn't the world be up in arms? Shouldn't they be rescued? But no other countries stepped in to help them. There was talk, but nothing more. Perhaps there were plans being made that no one knew about, a secret way to be rid of the Germans and rescue the Jews in the Netherlands. *Just not yet,* they said to one another, but as time went on they wondered, *When?* The fear of the future was growing in the gardens all through the city, a terror so deep that no one picked the flowers, for perhaps in this new world even that might be considered a crime.

One night, Margot decided that she and Anne would be more organized and happier if each made a list of all that needed to be done on the following day. Every day would be a day like any other if they wrote it all down, the classes they would attend, the friends they would see, the chores they must do. They both got into their beds with paper and pen, but Anne was uninterested in her sister's list of daily chores and activities, and instead decided to make her own list of all the things she wanted to do when the war was over.

Visit Omi in Switzerland. Stand in a garden of white roses. Travel to Paris when the chestnut trees were blooming. See New York, especially Radio City Music Hall and the great department store Macy's, owned by her father's friend's family. Walk down Hollywood Boulevard and place her hands on top of the handprints of the movie stars to see if they fit, especially Norma Shearer's, who had the leading role in the film version of Romeo and Juliet. *Have pierced ears and own a dozen pairs of earrings. Have her nails painted red. Watch the moon rise in America with her father standing beside her. Have her mother tell her she was beautiful. Fall in love. Live in a country where you could be free.*

"I made a to-do list," Margot said. "You made a wish list."

"You don't have wishes?"

It took a while before Margot spoke. "I'm afraid to."

"I'm not," Anne said.

"That's why you're you," Margot told her sister, and for the first time Anne wondered if her sister might be envious of her. She got into bed with Margot so she would not be so alone. She could see the black moth, so she closed her eyes.

"Once upon a time," Anne said, "there were two sisters. One was beautiful and one was not."

Margot laughed. "No, that's not the way the story goes."

"How does it go?"

Their voices were soft so that no one else could hear them. "Once upon a time, there were two sisters who would do anything for each other," Margot began.

"What would they do?" Anne's voice was softer than usual. She didn't feel very grown up now.

"They would protect each other and they would always believe in each other."

"No matter what?" Anne asked.

"No matter what," Margot told her.

"Then that's what I wish," Anne said.

"You don't have to wish." Margot's eyes were closed now too. "It's already true."

When her sister had fallen asleep, Anne crept from her bed to look out into the darkness in the courtyard. She wanted to believe they could protect each other, but they were living in wolf time, a time of shadows. Most people told themselves that all would be well, but if they stayed up late, if they really thought about it, they would know that no matter who loved you, no matter who tried to protect you, nothing was fine and nothing was the same, and by the end of May, all the rabbits were gone.

✶ ✶ ✶

It was Anne's eleventh birthday on the 12th of June. It had always been her lucky day, the best day of the year. Usually her friends gathered for games and cake. Last year she'd had eight friends at the celebration, including Hanneli and Sanne, but this year only the family celebrated. Still, eleven was a good age, and next year would be even better, and thirteen would be best of all.

"I can't wait to be grown up," Anne told Oma.

Her grandmother told her not to rush things. "When you are young," Oma said, "time goes slowly, and when you are old, you want to reverse time and go backward."

"I won't," Anne assured her grandmother. "I'll never want to go backward."

"Why do you want to grow up so fast?" Oma wanted to know. "Stay a child. Enjoy it."

Anne flung her arms around her grandmother, but she knew what she wanted, and she wanted to grow up more than she wanted anything. In her dreams, she was a grown woman and could do as she pleased. *California* was such a beautiful word, and she often repeated it to herself until she fell asleep as the moonlight poured through the window, a pale silvery light that made everything look unfamiliar in her own room, as if she was already living someplace brand new. Anne was certain she could be an actress, for even now she felt as if she was acting out a play every day, pretending to be someone she wasn't. The young girl who didn't know that the world was closing in on them, who didn't see her mother watching her to see if she would make a mistake, wrong shoes, wrong socks, wrong words when she answered a question. She kept her worries inside, and wasn't that acting? Was she not pretty enough, smart enough, brave enough? She had been in school plays and in holiday performances and was always the star of every show. The reason was simple: She could become someone else in the blink of an eye. She could be Juliet, she could be a witch in the forest, she could be a lost girl begging for bread, she could be Esther, the queen who had saved the Jews.

"How do you do it?" Anne's friend Hanneli asked her. They had been playing in Hanneli's room, acting out scenes from the movies they loved. Hanneli admired Anne's talents and was never jealous of her or annoyed by her the way some of the girls at school were. Unlike the other girls, she didn't mind if Anne always wanted to be the star.

"You're so different when you play the part of someone else," Hanneli said admiringly.

Anne shrugged, for she had no answer. It was difficult to explain how easy it was for her to become a character in a play, much easier than living her ordinary life. Maybe she was able to do so because she wished that she was someone else. The perfect sister, that was a part she would love to play, that was who she often wished to be, not that she'd ever admit it. The beautiful, kind sister everyone loved and admired and who always knew the right thing to say and do, who was generous rather than bossy, who all the boys gazed at with interest, who pleased her mother with everything she did. Anne had certainly studied Margot well enough; she could walk and talk like her, imitating her sister to amuse her friends and make them laugh. Or perhaps she could be someone else entirely, someone she'd never known and had wholly invented. She could be Merle Oberon, or the wonderful and mysterious actress Greta Garbo.

"You'll fit right into Hollywood."

"I don't know." Lately, Anne had been doubting her own dreams. "You have to be beautiful, and I'm not," she blurted.

She had been stung when she'd overheard the other girls

in her class discussing her. She was too sure of herself, they said, and too needy, both bossy and clingy. What hurt most of all was when she heard them say she wasn't half as attractive as Margot. Margot was a true beauty, they said, and Anne was only average. She knew it, of course, but the cruelty of their laughter cut right through her.

"All I know is that when you're in a play, you're the only one people watch. You're the one who shines," Hanneli told her friend.

It was true; more boys had begun to gather around Anne in the schoolyard, not because she was beautiful, but because she shimmered, like a firefly. She was so alive they were drawn to her, and they didn't even know why. She was electric, so much more intense than most people.

"Let's plan our lives in California," Anne said. "We'll swim in the Pacific Ocean every morning. We'll have chocolate cake and champagne." The girls looked at each other and laughed at the thought of being old enough to drink champagne.

"I'll live in your guesthouse," Hanneli declared. "Every movie star has one. I'll hide out there so I never have to leave."

"Never," Anne agreed.

All of a sudden, Hanneli looked solemn. Not everyone lived in a dream life. "If something happens and I don't get to go with you, promise me you'll write me letters."

Anne wondered if she shouldn't have spoken of her dreams to Hanneli. These were her most private thoughts and she now felt she'd revealed too much of herself. If her friends knew her real self, they would know she was selfish sometimes and that she felt she was different and special on occasion, but at other times she felt exactly the opposite, as if she was nothing more than a shadow on the wall. At night the room filled with moths, more and more all the time, until it was so dark it was impossible to see.

Otto Frank continued to write letters trying to get them out of the Netherlands, but as he wrote there was a dark cast of fear on his face. He said nothing about the fact that letters were taking longer and longer to get to where they'd been addressed, and that letters coming to him took weeks. He paced as he thought about what he would write next. He had already begged his wife's brothers to do anything they could. The situation was changing by the day, and was worse all the time. More and more rules were passed, depriving Jews of their livelihoods and their dignity. Lately, Anne couldn't see any farther than the green square, which had always felt as though it belonged to them. In the past, they had never thought twice about going out in the dusk, riding their bicycles or playing hide-and-seek, ducking beneath the bushes or watching the stars in the sky.

The simple things they'd taken for granted were no longer possible. Anne wished she could stand out in the square as night sifted down, which she and Pim used to do. The last time they'd done so seemed so long ago she could barely remember the bowl of stars above them. She wished she could walk along the canals in the evening and find a boat and row to the sea. If she tried hard enough, perhaps she could find a place where she could do as she pleased, where she wouldn't have to be afraid of the soldiers on the street; she would find a city far from here where she could spend all day in a bookstore and curl up and sleep there at night. When she closed her eyes, there she was, somewhere in the future where she didn't have to explain herself to anyone.

* * *

Anne and Margot sat outside on the steps of 37 Merwedeplein, not speaking, but sitting so close they could feel each other's hearts beating. More and more often the sisters looped their arms around each other's waists for comfort when they were both distressed. They had never been close, and they still didn't confide in each other. There was something Anne wanted that Margot couldn't give her, something she needed, a person who could understand her at the deepest level, soul to soul. And yet something had changed between them, for Anne knew she could trust Margot, who was honest and kindhearted, in a way she trusted no one else. Margot would never tell anyone that sometimes, as they sat outside on the steps in the shadow of the Skyscraper building, Anne cried, then wiped her eyes, embarrassed. "Something was in my eye," she always told her sister.

"It must be dust or a piece of grass," Margot would agree, even though she knew the truth.

Today when they sat on the steps, Anne didn't cry. She was learning to hold more and more of her feelings inside. Sometimes she imagined that if she didn't let them out in some way they might burst inside her.

"Are you all right?" Margot asked, because her sister was so quiet.

"Is anyone?" Anne found herself saying.

"You're answering a question with a question," Margot chided her gently.

Anne didn't take the opportunity to make their conversation into a joke, saying *Am I?* Instead, she whispered, "I know," and they sat even closer together.

When all the lights had been turned off and dusk had settled, Anne gazed up to scan the trees. There were so few birds; something had chased them away, a sense of doom, the weight of the silence in the city. The only birds that appeared to have stayed on were the magpies, since their kind never migrated far from home.

Margot pointed upward to the branches above them. "Isn't that the bird who follows you?"

Anne thought Margot was humoring her, but when she looked up, she saw that her sister was right. It was the same bird in the tree above them, the one who recognized her and followed her home from school. Anne stood up and waved him away. She wanted him to flee to Spain or Morocco and forget all about Amsterdam. She wanted him to be somewhere safe where the bombs didn't shake the stars in the sky.

"Go on," she called out. "Fly away now!"

When the magpie soared off above the elm trees, both sisters applauded, even though they knew they should be quiet so as not to call attention to themselves. They were so very different, but they were sisters all the same. You can love someone who doesn't understand you. That's what Anne had decided. You can trust them more than anyone else. Margot had on her favorite blue dress, one she would wear until it was threadbare. Before long, there would be no new dresses to buy and no money to buy them with, but they didn't know that now. In other times, girls of their ages went to dances, they fell in love, they prepared to go to universities, they walked along the canals and didn't have to show their identification cards, they were not in mortal fear, they kissed their parents good night, they went to bed and weren't afraid of their own dreams, they didn't cry and pretend not to, they didn't wish that all the birds would fly away to a safe place that was far from here, they didn't wish they could follow them.

✳ ✳ ✳

Anne had begun to dream of monsters. Each one had a human face and long arms and legs. They pinched her in her dreams and bruised her arms and legs. The monsters spoke German and they scratched at the window, leaving their fingerprints on the glass. They were only in her imagination, she knew that, but she had begun to fear going to sleep. In the mornings when she woke, she saw the black moth in the corner, larger than it had been before.

Everyone in the family noticed that Anne wasn't her usual cheerful self. She was so quiet it was sometimes possible to forget she was there, and that wasn't like Anne at all. She was usually impossible to ignore and, if anything, took up too much space. Now she was quiet, thinking things over, wondering if the life they'd led before had been nothing more than a dream.

When her mother sent Anne to the market, she overheard people talking about *the Jews*. She was behind them and was too afraid to pass them. She felt a pulse in her throat. "We won't have to suffer with them around much longer," one woman said to her friend. She was an ordinary woman wearing a gray coat. Anne took a breath and forced herself to walk past the women. She walked as fast as she could, but when the woman spied Anne, she made a face. This woman was a goblin, just like the figures in her dreams, only she was here, wearing a gray coat, a scarf at her throat. Anne walked even faster. "Who does she think she is?" the woman said. She spoke in a well-mannered voice, but the hatred was there, just underneath her words.

"Ugly little thing," the other woman said, but by then Anne was running back to 37 Merwedeplein.

Otto was at his desk writing letters when she arrived home. Right away, he knew his daughter was distressed, and he left his desk to go to her. "Did something happen?"

When she explained how the women had acted toward her, Otto shook his head.

"Am I different from other people?" Anne asked her father. "What do they have against me?"

"They've been taught to hate, and unfortunately, we're the object of that hate," Pim told her. "It's not personal."

"But it's not fair," Anne said. "It shouldn't be this way."

She ran upstairs to the rooftop, where she could be alone. What she'd experienced on the street felt deeply personal to her, no matter what Pim said. On this day, she felt as if she knew nothing of the world. Anything could happen. People could betray you and surprise you, they could hate you for no reason, whether or not it was fair. She sat under the clear blue sky, and there was the magpie who had followed her home. "Fly away," she told the bird when he landed on the rooftop, but he stayed where he was, he didn't fly away to Morocco or to Spain, and so they stayed there together, for the truth was, there was really nowhere else to go.

What We Lost

We were not citizens and had no rights. There was no country to escape to, none would have us, none wanted us, none came to our rescue. We could not go out at night or raise our eyes when we passed soldiers on the street corners. We could not smile or laugh in public, and if we did, our mothers hushed us and tugged on our coats. Remember, they were telling us, we are living behind locked doors.

In our country everything was the same and everything had changed. The canals were there, and the trees, and our apartments, but the things we had taken for granted seemed like treasures to us now: books, bread, cake, aunts and uncles, cousins, a holiday, a river, a future.

When we looked in the mirror, we didn't understand why they didn't see what we saw. Why were we considered to be so different? Were we not like them?

That was when we began to wonder how much longer we would be safe.

PART THREE

Unspoken
Amsterdam, December 1940–May 1941

There were certain things they never talked about. They never mentioned the future or the past. Only a few words of doubt or fear might cause the monsters to appear right in front of them, walking along the road or there in their very own bedroom, sitting in the closet or waiting under their beds, counting every breath they took. They had been in nightmares once upon a time, but now the monsters were real, flesh and blood, wearing heavy boots and thick jackets.

The girls closed their eyes and wished away all that was evil. But monsters prefer silence, they delight in quiet houses and desperate people. *They take whatever they want while no one says a word. They steal people's souls and keep them in a satchel that they carry over their shoulders.*

That was when the younger sister realized that the monsters would be there whether or not they spoke of them. She crawled into her sister's bed. She took a breath and then she said the truth out loud.

All we have to do is open our eyes. Then we'll see what has happened.

They're at the window right now.

CHAPTER FIVE

Snow was falling and a sheen of blue ice covered the ground. Just below the surface of the frozen canals silvery fish were motionless, shining like stars, dreaming through the coldest months of the year. Anne's favorite thing to do in winter was to skate at the ice rink where she took figure skating lessons or with her friends on the frozen ponds of Vondelpark, the huge park of a hundred twenty acres in the center of Amsterdam. When she was skating, the world seemed full of joy, and she and her friends laughed and teased one another as if it was any other winter; they wore gloves and mittens and glided along in a row as if they were figure skaters.

"Faster," Anne always called out, and they went so fast they were nearly flying.

Hanne and Sanne and Anne locked arms and laughed until they thought they might fall onto the ice.

"We can't go any faster than this," Hanneli declared.

"How do we know if we don't try? Maybe we could set a record if someone timed us," Anne said, which was why her friends loved her, even if she could be difficult. She always thought bigger than anyone else.

There were sirens echoing in the city, but the girls ignored them, they barely heard them. All the same, they felt shivers down their spines. At last, they stopped skating so they would have time to get home before dark. The world appeared different now that it wasn't a blur as they sped over the ice. They thought they were shivering in the cold, but that wasn't it at all. Fear has a way of staying with you, even when you tell yourself you're safe. Their parents were watching them and whispering to one another, and if the girls looked carefully, if they squinted their eyes, they could see the soldiers beyond the trees. They had sharp teeth that they kept hidden. They never once smiled. But they watched from a distance and every single one carried a rifle.

Jews were being harassed on the streets more and more

frequently, as the Dutch Nazis were making their presence felt. Still, the girls stayed out until their fingers and toes had nearly turned blue, enjoying every minute. They were young and the ice was perfect, and the days when they skated felt like little miracles. They went so fast it was almost as if they could disappear, high into the crystalline sky.

* * *

On cold winter evenings, the Frank family gathered inside for dinner as ice formed on the windowpanes. They played Monopoly or cards. The grown-ups listened to the radio, trying to get news from the outside world, but soon enough, listening to the BBC in London was nearly impossible. The only news that was allowed were local broadcasts controlled by the Nazis, the sort of news you couldn't trust. Pim turned off the radio then; he got his news from friends after that, relying on people who had connections within the Resistance who told the truth, reporting what was happening in occupied Poland, where the Jews were under German control, where they were beaten and robbed on the streets, the men's beards cut off to humiliate them before being forced to turn somersaults and then to get down on their knees for acts of mercy that never came. In Poland, 3.3 million Jews were residents in 1939, and by the end of the war little more than three hundred and fifty thousand survived.

Oma went to bed right after dinner. She was cold all the time now and she wore a sweater and two shawls. On some nights she didn't speak at all. "Pay no attention to me," Oma said whenever she was asked if something was wrong. The truth was, everything was so wrong she didn't know where to begin. She knew she was ill, the signs were all there, her labored breathing, the pain in her side, but she didn't wish to upset anyone. What good would it do to complain? "Enjoy your games," she told the family when they asked her if she'd like to join in. "Old ladies go to bed early."

But it was something more, and Anne knew it. She brewed the last of the blue tea and brought Oma a cup. Oma would no longer talk about the future when Anne asked her opinion. "Do you think I know what will come?" Oma said. "Anne, I know nothing, and I can change nothing. If I could, I would have made certain I was born in another time and place. I'd take you with me, into the future. I'd take us all far from here."

If you looked into her eyes, it seemed that Oma knew more than she was letting on, but she would not say another word. She was folded in on herself, rarely leaving her bed. Before Anne put the deck of cards away, she drew two cards for luck. She would tell her own fortune if no one else could. She wanted a queen or an ace, which seemed like lucky cards, but instead she drew a ten and a three. She kept those cards under her pillow. Anne had not been raised as a religious Jew; she came from a modern family who had considered themselves to be German until the Nazis came to power. Anne didn't know the meaning of ten in Hebrew, that Abraham was willing to undergo ten trials to prove his love of God, that there were ten plagues in Egypt and ten miracles in the Temple. She had no idea that the number three meant completeness and that the earth was created on that day.

She was considered a child now, she could only do as she was told, she had to put her dreams away. All the same, she had hope for the future. Things would change once she grew up.

✷　✷　✷

In the first week of December, Otto Frank moved the company's headquarters into a narrow 17th-century brick building in an area along the canals at 263 Prinsengracht. In the courtyard next door, a huge chestnut tree grew. It reminded Anne of the one that had been at the Montessori school, and she was happy to see another tree that might grant wishes, though she decided to wait for a truly special wish before she asked for anything. The Prinsengracht area seemed magical, even if it was a business district and rather shabby. Anne sometimes went with her father to his office. She loved walking along the canal on the old brick sidewalks that were so narrow that she and her father often had to walk in single file. The canals were so beautiful, framed by tall, regal elm trees that had been planted in the 17th century.

Anne's father was busy with his partners, as they tried their best to make the business successful even in such difficult times. He didn't know how long he would be able to keep the company, for it was rumored that Jewish businesses would be taken over by the government. To be safe, he might have to transfer the business into the names of his two trusted partners, Johannes Kleiman and Victor Kugler, who weren't

Jewish. Miep and Bep, the two office assistants, were there to help look after the business as well. Anne looked forward to seeing Miep every time she accompanied her father to work, for she had become almost a part of the Frank family, beloved by all. Anne enjoyed chatting with Bep, who was the youngest, about movies and boys. Miep often allowed Anne to test the various recipes that had to be thickened with Opekta, the ingredient Pim's company sold to ensure that homemade jam was as good as anything that had been store-bought. Many people made their own preserves now, using bruised fruit from the market or whatever grew in their own small gardens and had been saved for the winter in their cellars, kept cold in baskets or jars. Blackberry jam was Anne's favorite. Apple was next.

Whenever she was left alone in her father's office, Anne read a book if she'd brought one with her. She had begun to understand that a writer's work was a private act, one in which the writer was in touch with the deepest portion of her soul, the part shown to no one else. The stories Anne loved to read best were fairy tales that took place deep in the forest where people could be lost or saved, they could find what they wanted most in life, or lose everything and everyone they'd ever loved. They could go so deeply into the dark woods where they would never be found. They would aways make certain to leave a trail of breadcrumbs to lead them home.

* * *

Anne seemed her old self whenever she went to Hanneli's house, where they often played with her friend's baby sister, Gabi. The girls made Gabi laugh as they dressed her up in hats and scarves, and she was so well-behaved they forgot that she could often be annoying.

"Once upon a time," Anne told Gabi, "there was a moth that no one could see."

They were drinking the hot chocolate that Hanneli's mother had made for them. It didn't taste the way hot chocolate used to taste, it was thinner and watery, but delicious all the same.

"Because they didn't want to see it. But it was there all the same. Night and day. It was waiting."

Hanneli looked nervous and came to sit closer. "Waiting for what?" she asked.

"For the right time to be free."

"Where will the people be?" Hanneli asked.

"Under their beds!"

The girls let out a cry and slipped under Hanneli's bed, taking the baby with them. The room looked so empty from this vantage point. They breathed softly.

"Are the moths going to come now?" Hanneli asked.

"Someday, but not today," Anne said.

"Good," Hanneli said, for the spell had been broken. "We don't want to share our hot chocolate with them."

The girls laughed and crawled out from beneath the bed and Anne was relieved when they went back to playing dress-up with Gabi. She wasn't ready to share her fears, not even with her closest friends. She kept that part of herself secret. It was the part that knew the black moths would arrive on the day all the people were gone.

* * *

The new year had always been a hopeful time when bonfires were lit on the canals and skaters stayed out until midnight, a night when the future had always been filled with possibility.

But this year the streets were dark and the doors of houses and apartments were locked. January was the month when it was announced that all Jewish residents, including those who had one Jewish parent or a single Jewish grandparent, had to register with the Civic Registry or face five years in prison. Nearly a hundred and sixty thousand men and women did so, lining up, wearing their boots and their heaviest coats, giving their names and addresses, even though many were uncomfortable doing so. They looked grim as they waited at government offices to be counted among those who were not considered worthy of having the rights of human beings.

It was nothing more than procedure, they were told, a way to simplify matters should they need to be contacted. Nearly everyone complied. They were counted and numbered, they were written down in the official documents, name, age, and address. And that was it, they had become fish in a net, they were already drowning, only they didn't know it yet. All they were told was misinformation, lies wrapped in a Nazi edict. *Follow the rules and no one will be hurt. Do as we say and you will be fine.* After all the information was written down, the authorities knew where to find the Jews, they knew how many children were in a family and what their ages were, they knew if there were old people, worthless in a work camp, they knew who lived in the nicer neighborhoods and were likely to have good silverware and jewelry. It was all written down now and kept on file, and that file was locked with a key that might as well have been made of bones. Jews were considered to be *something* rather than *someone*.

The goblins knew where they were, they had a list and a plan, they had secrets, and they had all the time in the world.

✳ ✳ ✳

What had happened in Germany and Austria and Poland seemed closer all the time. In that same month of January, the membership of the Dutch Nazi party swelled. More and more riots on the streets broke out and Jewish men were beaten and arrested for no reason. Gatherings of Jews were now held in secret, and people were more cautious all the time. You could be arrested for just about anything, and the rules changed and became more severe by the day.

One cannot know the future, and it was impossible then to suspect that the Netherlands would have the greatest

percentage of Jews murdered of any western European country by the end of the war.

Otto and Edith decided to keep the deeply disturbing
news of what was happening from their daughters, but their
discussions filtered through the walls. In apartments such
as theirs, arguments echoed. Anne understood that this new
year was different from all the others she had known, but a
year was only twelve months long, and wasn't it possible that
the next year would be better? She wanted to be more like
Pim, who was always so positive. She mostly succeeded and
went about living her life, but when the lights were out and
she was in bed, she thought she still spied the black moth in
the corner of her room. What kept it alive? Did it drink water
from the tap in the bathroom? Did it unravel sweaters and
scarves and feed upon the woolen threads? Did it nest on the
ceiling, so silent that their boarder passed by without notic-
ing it? Anne raised her hand to see if the moth would come to
her, but it had already disappeared. Of course she must have
imagined it, she was sure of it, such creatures didn't exist,
moths were never that big, as large as a bat, they were not
waiting in the closet or beneath your bed.

All the same, Anne slept with her head under the blanket, and her breathing was soft, as if she was still hiding even in her sleep. She was like hundreds of other girls of her age in the Netherlands, afraid of what they might find when they awoke. Anne didn't think about California anymore; it seemed much too far away. It seemed like a place in a fairy tale to her now, not a real destination where people went shopping and were able to leave their houses whenever they pleased without fear of the German police. She was here and nowhere else. She was in her own room, in her own bed, living the one life that she had. She decided she would wait until their situation was better before she thought about the future. In the morning, the light would be bright enough to melt the snow on the window ledges, and all that had happened in the dark would seem like nothing more than a bad dream.

CHAPTER SIX

The sisters awoke early, even though it was Sunday, when they usually slept late. It was February 16, Margot's fifteenth birthday.

"Do you feel different?" Anne asked her sister.

Margot laughed softly. "Not at all. Am I supposed to?"

"Of course you are. You're supposed to feel different every year."

Margot looked grown up, she was almost a woman, and she had decided to put aside foolish things like parties, but Otto and Edith had decided to give her the best celebration they could. Their brilliant, well-behaved elder daughter always tried to do her best, never asking for much in return, and she deserved to be happy despite their circumstances, at least for an afternoon. Margot was delighted with the celebration they had that day, thrilled with her gifts. It was a tradition for Pim to present his daughters with a birthday poem or letter that he had written, and this year was no different. *On this, your day,* he wrote, *We wish you happiness in every way.*

"You were right," Margot told Anne as the girls washed up after lunch. "I'm different."

Margot had tears in her eyes, and Anne couldn't understand why she would be sad about growing up. It was all that Anne wanted.

"You think you want it until you have it," Margot said. "There are so many things I'll never do again."

"Childish, silly things. Now your life is out there waiting for you," Anne assured her.

When Margot looked at her, her kind, dark eyes shone with pity, and Anne felt foolish without knowing exactly why.

"What do you think is out there?" Margot asked.

"Everything!"

Their parents were in the parlor, arguing over the money Otto had spent on gifts and books. "You think you can fix everything with presents?" they heard their mother say.

Margot turned to hug Anne, even though her hands were

wet. "I always hope you're right," she said, and Anne hugged her back even though she could feel the darkness wrapping its arms around them. *Let us grow up to be who we want to be,* she thought. *Let us go out and find everything. Let us see stars and planets and countries that are far away. Let us be women, let us be sisters, let us always celebrate.*

One week after Margot's birthday, a riot began at an ice cream parlor called Koco, a gathering place for Jews, where refugees drank coffee while they talked politics. There had been riots before, but this was different, it was far more brutal and there were lasting consequences. After a mob of Dutch Nazis came to harass the owners and patrons and damage the restaurant, a team of German police came next. The customers had anticipated an attack would take place, and they had been prepared for a fight, but they had expected Dutch authorities, not the ferocious German police who came to defeat them at any cost. There had been days of random violence leading up to this one, and now it had exploded.

As a reprisal, more than four hundred Jewish men had randomly been arrested, then deported to Mauthausen, a concentration camp so inhumane only two of those taken into custody on that day survived.

"This is madness," Edith said when she heard about the arrests. "You're an honest man. There's no reason to arrest you," she told her husband.

Anne and Margot linked hands, but they didn't look at each other.

"Girls, do not worry," Pim said in a soft voice. "Your mother is right. We'll be fine."

All the same, that night the girls slept in the same bed knowing that there were Jewish children all over the city who had lost their fathers and brothers.

＊　＊　＊

After the night of the riot, the gates to random violence were thrown open. What happened once can happen again, even if you lock your doors, even if you're honest and fair and have obeyed all the rules. Rules change, they're broken so easily it seemed they'd been made of paper or thread. Jews were attacked every day, at times when it was least expected. They were grabbed off bicycles or beaten while walking down the street.

These were days when children looked up at the sky and couldn't see the sun. Anne sat out on the roof as often as she could, and there, above the streets of her neighborhood, she imagined other worlds and thought of the stories Pim so often told her and Margot, tales in which good people were rewarded and those who were evil suffered and never won. Sometimes she didn't even notice when a moth landed beside her. There wasn't just one anymore and they didn't appear only in the dark, in corners where no one bothered to look.

They were everywhere now.

Otto once again turned to his old friend Charley Straus. Straus had promised to help the Frank family, and Pim was depending on his friend, who thankfully was a man of character, as well as a person whose voice mattered to the US government. The two friends had remained close, but

even Straus, who was so well-connected, was having diffi-
culty helping his friend. There was a quota of immigrants
allowed into the States, regardless of their faith, and no one
above that number could enter, no matter how horrifying
their circumstances might be. A few years earlier, a boatload
of Jewish refugees from Germany had been turned away in
Havana, Cuba, and then the US government refused to allow
the ship entry as well, even though many of the passengers
returned to the deaths that awaited them in Europe. No
country wanted Jewish refugees.

Pim had applied for emigration visas at the American
consulate in Rotterdam back in 1938, but the information he'd
sent had been destroyed. There had been a conference that
year in Evian, France, and although all countries represented
expressed compassion for the plight of the Jews fleeing persecution from the Nazis, most countries, including the United
States, declined to allow refugees to enter. Even in 1939, the
waiting list to immigrate to the States contained three hundred thousand names.

The loss of Otto's official papers in the bombing of
Rotterdam that were needed to legally emigrate was a huge

setback, and time was running out. Sometimes it seemed there was no time at all, as if it was all vanishing in the dark so quickly that hours became minutes and weeks were no longer than a single day. Leaving Europe had become a life-and-death matter.

We don't have much time. They're after all of us. I know you can do this for me, for my family, and I will be in your debt forevermore.

"Charley will get us to New York," Anne overheard her father assure her mother after he wrote to his friend. "It just takes time."

"Really? You still think he can? Then where are the tickets?" Edith wanted to know. "How long can we wait?" Edith was no longer sure about anything. "We don't have the kind of money we need." It could take thousands to pay for visas for each member of the family, let alone their travels, money they simply didn't have. "And soon enough, it will be impossible."

"It will happen!" Otto insisted. "Charley has access to people in Washington. And your brothers will petition for us."

Edith's brothers were in Massachusetts, a good thing, for if you wished to enter the States a close relative had to be willing to vouch for you and promise to give you a home and a job once you arrived. But they had no means yet to support their sister and her family, and who would pay the emigration fees, which were ridiculously high, almost five thousand dollars a person? Once that was done the visas needed to be processed and stamped at the American consulate in Rotterdam and then sent out. Anne knew her father, and as she stood in the corridor, she could hear the doubt in his voice as he argued with Edith. When Pim looked over and realized that his younger daughter had overheard a conversation not meant for her ears, he called out in what he hoped was a more cheerful tone. "Nothing to worry about. We'll figure it out."

But if that was true, why didn't Pim sound like himself? Why could Anne hear so much fear beneath his words?

"We'll go to New York or Boston," her father vowed. "It's only a matter of time."

"And then on to California?" Anne said in a small voice. It was the way you said things when you didn't really believe in them anymore.

"Then wherever we please," Pim said. Her dear father, who was always so kindhearted and generous, who believed in the best in people, now couldn't look at his own daughter for fear she'd see the truth in his eyes. She saw it anyway. Nothing was certain.

"We can hope," Pim said.

No one could argue with that. Hope was all they had now.

* * *

In April 1941, Otto Frank wrote to his friend Charley Straus in New York. "I would not ask if conditions here would not force me to do all I can in time to be able to avoid worse," Pim wrote. "It is for the sake of the children mainly that we have to care for. Our own fate is of less importance."

Charley was in Washington, DC, however, and didn't receive Otto's letter when it arrived. But once he did, Charley and Edith's brothers did everything possible to help. Otto continued to do his best to figure out how to get the visas that would allow his family to leave the Netherlands. It seemed he never stopped. He was often too busy to have a conversation or read one of his beloved books. The process was becoming more and more difficult. Soon, there were changes in US regulations that meant new paperwork.

* * *

Time continued to slip away, and Pim had begun to feel hopeless, though he continued to hide his fears from his children. Often at dinner they spoke about all they would do when they reached America, even though Otto wondered when and if that would ever happen. They made lists and argued over whether or not they should go to Massachusetts, where Edith's brothers lived, or to New York, the city Otto knew so well. "First stop, Macy's department store," Pim always insisted.

It seemed as if nothing had changed for the family, but one morning, when everyone else was asleep, Anne heard her father crying behind a locked door, just as Oma sometimes did when she thought no one was home. He was in the toilet, the water running in an attempt to hide his sobs. Anne sat down in the hallway, in the dark, and later she didn't ask her father any questions, but she knew the truth. This was the way you learned about the world your parents thought they were protecting you from. You found out on your own. You looked and you saw what was behind everything they told you. Anne knew that her mother had hidden her gold earrings and a necklace given to her on her eighteenth birthday in a jar beneath the sink. That was not what you did when you felt safe in your own house. That was not what you did when you had faith in the future. Her father, who had believed that good would win out, had lost hope. It had vanished and there was nothing he could do to get it back. Everything was changing, step by step, like a wolf walking in the woods, in silence, in the shadows, alone in the dark.

It was a year of last things, of endings and losses, a year when you had to think on your feet, a time when it was best to appreciate the smallest things, things you might lose in the future, the small joys in life, sunlight, a black cat, a book to read at night in bed. Pim sat in his chair for hours, no longer reading his beloved novels. He was quiet in the evenings, and when he came home from work, he seemed exhausted. Anne noticed that her parents no longer quarreled. But one night, when Anne crept downstairs, she saw that her mother and father were both in the kitchen, drinking tea and not speaking a word to each other. They were two ghosts in the same room; they were people who no longer had anything to say to each other. That was when Anne realized that there were times when silence was worse than an argument.

Life became smaller. People stopped talking about the future. It was enough to try to get through the here and now. When you were an outcast, you only talked to people you knew. You kept to yourself. You made certain to speak quietly when you were outside, or not to speak at all. Beautiful girls made themselves look plain; they wore gray clothes and no makeup and they didn't lift their eyes when they passed by the soldiers. Women left their babies home alone rather than taking them into the street, where they might be grabbed from their arms. People waited for the next laws against the Jews the way farmers wait for a storm. You knew it was coming, as if the wind had risen from the east, and you expected that blasts of rain would soon begin to fall, but you never knew when the storm would strike. Perhaps it would pass over you; you had hoped that it might, until you lost that hope. Perhaps you would be saved from what was to come, even though you saw it coming closer all the time.

Anne was sitting on the steps when she saw it happen. It was the day she realized it wasn't hope that they needed, it was bravery. A small storm, a circle of disaster, a portent of what was and what was to come. It was a spring day and there was a haze of green as gardens began to grow. But despite the warm weather, it seemed as if the storm had dropped down from the sky onto the grass. Anne thought what she spied was a cloud of black moths in the square just across the way, but it was a boy, spinning around, looking for an escape. A Jewish student, he had been walking home until he was suddenly surrounded by a group of Dutch children. He was eight or nine and Anne didn't know him by name. Still, she recognized him. She thought she'd seen him at the ice cream shop with his father. He was smaller than the other children around him. He was carrying a satchel of books and wore a hat that had probably belonged to an older brother or his father, for it was too big and slipped down over his eyes.

"We caught a Jew," the children cried as they circled him. They were fair-haired and in their school clothes; some were older than Anne, a few were teenagers there with their younger brothers. They were looking for trouble, and now they had found it. The Dutch schoolboys were circling the boy in the hat, coming closer to him all the time. It was such a warm day it almost seemed like summer. The Jewish boy's mother must have feared he'd catch a chill. *Wear a coat just in case*, she'd likely told him. She surely loved him more than life itself. The leaves on the huge elm trees in the city were budding green. Once people had come here from the places you had to run away from, where there was death and destruction, where some people weren't considered human. It was still the same city, except now you could almost see the underworld beneath the grass, the fires that burned there, the soot and heat.

Anne looked at the boy and he stared back across the distance between them. They lived in a land without birds, a country in which there were no laws that would protect them, a place where it wasn't possible to be a child anymore. That life was over. It was impossible now. Anne and the boy had never met, but that didn't matter, they understood each other perfectly. There were thousands of them, unprotected children all through the neighborhoods and on every street of the city; they were out in the countryside, they were on roads leading to the sea. Even if no one saw them, even if people in other countries lived as if the world was still the same, they now knew the truth. Even children understood what had happened. No one would protect them if they didn't protect one another.

When Anne cried out for the boy to run, that was exactly what he did.

What We Lost

In January, all Jews had registered with the government. We weren't welcome in air raid shelters if bombs were falling. Instead, we hid in the cellars, where rats gathered. We were made to carry papers marked with a J. We were not allowed to ride in cars when we lost a member of our family and had to walk to the funeral. We mourned in the streets. We wept in front of everyone.

The Jewish Council was created to keep order; they believed they were doing the right thing, complying, not realizing that the Germans can keep track of us through the council. They say it's to maintain order, but the truth is, now we are even more easily found if they want to arrest us.

Jewish residents have been registered with the government with name, age, and address. They were babies in their mothers' arms, they were beautiful girls and boys who were the best students in their classes. We stood in line, our eyes lowered.

People called us names we hadn't heard before, but we soon

learned that they all meant Jew. We were nothing to these people, not even human beings.

Our fathers cried in front of us.

Our mothers said we should have left long ago.

But where can we go? No country will take us. No one will have us.

The people who hate us have lists of our names and where we live. They know everything about us.

We think this is a story we have read before in fairy tales.

We think we won't have long before we have to hide.

PART FOUR

The World and the Underworld
Amsterdam, June 1941—February 1942

There were goblins that looked like handsome men and girls who had cried so many tears they could not open their eyes. There were women who dreamed they had turned into flowers, and flowers that turned to dust as soon as you tried to pick them.

Good people were hiding in the dark, peering out through the cracks in their doors.

They were supposed to stay inside, and the older sister did as she was told, but the younger one climbed onto the roof late at night. She wished she were a bird. She wanted to fly away, so she held out her arms, and the wind lifted her up. The sky was so dark she could barely see, but she saw enough. There were the monsters walking through the neighborhood, sitting on their steps, just waiting for them to wake up and come outside.

CHAPTER SEVEN

In the summer of 1941, Oma became seriously ill. She was pale and exhausted and often refused to eat. She insisted that nothing was wrong. "I'm fine, don't ask me again, don't worry about me." But Anne could hear her grandmother moaning in the middle of the night. When no one was home, Oma sat in a chair in the dining room. She looked out the window and cried even though she knew she was too old to cry. She was a grandmother and crying should only be for children and for young brokenhearted women; still, she had her reasons. She was ill and she knew it, but there were more important tragedies around her, ones so huge her own life and death meant little to her. By now she was certain that what had happened in her own country was also happening here. She could have answered Anne's question about what the future might be, but Anne hadn't asked again. Even children knew that they lived in a world in which it was dangerous to ask questions. If you did, you might just get the answers.

Although Oma didn't speak her fears aloud, her terror surfaced in small ways. Her voice was too soft to hear, she could not sleep, not even a wink, the portions she took for dinner were so small they would suit a bird, she was too wrapped up in the sorrow of what might come to notice that her granddaughter was standing quietly in the corridor, watching her, beginning to understand all that her grandmother wasn't able to say.

Oma grew so weak that at last Pim insisted she be taken to the hospital.

"I'm fine," Oma said. She had always kept her pain and her worries to herself. "Don't pay attention to me."

They called in a doctor who had been well-known and respected before the Nazis arrived, but now he was only allowed to have Jewish patients. He seemed ten years older than he had been when he was considered one of the best physicians in the city. When the doctor went house to house to see his patients, he didn't dare carry his medical bag for fear of being stopped and questioned. Instead of carrying his bag, he hid his stethoscope and thermometer, along with assorted dressings and bandages, in his coat pockets. He cried sometimes over all he had seen, knowing there was worse to come. He had witnessed German brutality firsthand, beaten men, women who had been taken against their will, people who were afraid to ask for anything, even a doctor's visit.

The doctor quickly examined Oma, and when the family saw the frown on his face, they understood the diagnosis was not good. Oma had been keeping secrets from them. The blood she coughed up. The chest pains that left her breathless. The doctor shook his head and put away his stethoscope.

"We have to go now," he told Pim. "She needs immediate treatment."

Right away they bundled up Oma, for she was cold even in summer. She told them not to bother, insisting that all she needed was a good night's sleep, a cup of tea, some soup. "This is completely unnecessary," she insisted, but they brought her to the Jewish Hospital, where surgery was done that same day. If it was cancer, no one said so out loud. When the family came to bring her home, they brought flowers with them, pale carnations that were a treasure. *She will love them*, they told one another. *The flowers will remind her of the beauty of the world*, they vowed, standing in the corridor that was so full of sick people some were on stretchers on the floor.

The doctor met them in the hall outside the surgery room. He had a blank expression that he had perfected during his many years of telling people bad news. He never said the word *incurable*, but it was there in his eyes. He was someone who had long ago realized that hope was the wrong thing to look for in this world. You needed to be brave; you needed to face whatever might come next. He sat up at nights remembering people who were no longer living. He had a notebook filled with their last words to him.

It was cold in the hospital corridor, and the Frank family huddled together. The sisters wished they were wearing their hats and their gloves.

"Rest is the best thing," the doctor told them. As soon as Edith heard this, she began to weep. She understood that the doctor was saying there was nothing more that could be done for her mother.

After Oma came home, Anne often sat beside her grandmother's bed in the dining room to read to her from the book of myths. Occasionally, when no one was around, she would tell her grandmother one of her own stories that she had written in invisible ink inside her mind. Maybe someday she would write them down, but for now they came alive as she told them to her grandmother. She wanted to transport Oma to a different world, one where anything was possible, even for an old woman who had trouble breathing, who could no longer get out of bed without help. Today she told her grandmother a story about a world where people were all good at heart.

"That's you," Oma declared. "You're the one who will do good in the world."

"No." Anne laughed. "Oma, it can't be. I'm selfish and rude. Everyone says so."

"Well, they're wrong. I'm your grandmother and I know who you are." Oma was upset when Anne spoke badly about herself. "You have always been special. Don't listen to them when they tell you that you have to be like everyone else."

Sitting there beside her beloved grandmother, Anne

wondered what people did when they lost the ones they loved most in the world. How did they ever get over their loss? Did they give up all hope or did they carry their loved ones with them, kept in their hearts? She wanted to be the person Oma believed she was. She wanted to do good in the world. She often held her grandmother's hand, waiting for Oma to fall asleep on these afternoons, and she did so now. Her grandmother's skin felt thin, as if it were vanishing. What would she do without her? Who in the world would know who she really was? But now, as her grandmother drifted off to sleep, she told Anne not to worry, she would be loved forevermore.

The fear was unspoken, but it was everywhere. Otto sat in the park so that he could be alone to cry. He blamed himself for not sending his children away to England when he had the chance. He wrote letter after letter, still trying to get the family out of the Netherlands. At last a letter arrived from Charley Straus. "Finally!" Pim was elated, and he waved the envelope in the air as if it were a treasure. "Girls," he cried out to his daughters. "It's here." The letter that they'd been waiting for. The possibility of going far from this place, as far as possible. Straus had been in communication with the National Refugee Service and said that the paperwork was all set to go for their visas.

Pim took his daughters' hands and drew them into a dance that made them all laugh. At last, he seemed happy again.

"New York," Margot said.

"California," Anne cried, remembering her dreams of the ocean and the wide boulevards and the life that was so far away, dreams she hadn't had for a long time.

"I told you he would help us," Otto said to his wife.

"Why shouldn't he?" Edith said. "Everyone should help us, but no one does."

When Margot went to bed that night, she saw that Anne had taken out her suitcase and was already packing. For the first time in a long time, they felt lucky. They felt young again.

"We don't know exactly when we're going. How do you know what you'll need?" she asked.

"I'm taking everything," Anne said.

"Maybe we should leave everything and start all over again."

Anne laughed and quickly agreed. "Yes, everything will be brand new!"

They danced, leaping on the beds, nearly flying across the room. They hoped to never again see their bedroom or the street where they lived once their papers arrived.

When Anne turned twelve, there wasn't much of a celebration. The house was kept quiet to make certain that Oma could get her rest. It was a house of whispers now, of sitting in the kitchen not speaking at dinnertime, of going to bed early while the sky was still light, of staying inside even though the parks were green. Margot hugged Anne close when she saw how disappointed her sister was that there were no festivities. They sat on the roof and Anne wished she could climb down and find herself anywhere but here.

"The next birthday will be better," Margot told her. "We have to remember how it used to be. It will be that way again. You don't have to worry. It will all change."

And yet, Anne dreamed about ogres; she looked beneath

their beds, frightened to go to sleep at night. She thought she heard the trees outside the windows whispering late at night, each branch filled with thorns. She imagined men climbing through their windows to steal her and her sister and carry them into the forest of bones, a place from which you never returned. She thought of Germany, and Austria, and occupied Poland, where bodies were buried in huge unmarked graves, where houses were emptied of all who had ever lived there. There were children all over the city who had the same dreams, and when they saw one another on the street, they knew that they all wished they could fly, that way no one would ever catch them. They would perch in trees, and they would sleep there too, far from the world around them, in a place where there were no monsters hidden under their beds, just waiting for them to close their eyes.

"We have to keep trying to leave," Otto said.

His words were hopeful, but he seemed rattled. Anne and Margot saw the look on their mother's face when she left the room. She hadn't said a word. Edith covered the clock in the parlor with a cloth napkin. She didn't want to see how little time they had left. Anne saw her sitting on her bed, not speaking, not even arguing, and unless Anne was mistaken, her mother was crying in the dark. Anne went in and sat beside her, and still Edith said nothing. Anne thought she would ignore her, but then her mother reached for her hand and they sat there together, holding on as best they could.

At last, Otto heard back from his friend Charley Straus in New York. "I have taken up the matter of your immigration to this country with the National Refugee Service. I have also discussed it with the State Department officials as I would very much like to help you. I am afraid the news is not good news." Without access to a US consulate, the Franks would not be able to go to America. The American consulate in Rotterdam had closed on June 30 and there were no more visas to be had.

It was the trying and failing that made Otto lock himself in his room. Anne sat in the hallway, her legs pulled up. The magpie was in his nest, right there in full view of everyone. *It's not safe*, Anne thought, and that thought made her cry. Margot had been reading in their room, and now she came out and when she spied Anne, she sank down beside her sister.

"Everyone has to cry sometimes," Margot whispered. She took Anne's hand and laced her fingers through her sister's. "Even parents."

It was true, and they both knew it, but it didn't make them feel any better as they sat in the hallway.

"Come on," Margot said, and they rose to their feet and ran outside to the balcony, where the sun was so bright they had to shade their eyes, and the leaves on the trees were so green they might have been anywhere at all.

* * *

At last, there was a day when real joy could be celebrated. Miep was to be married, and it was as if a member of the Frank family was about to be wed. Miep had promised Anne she would be the very first guest to be invited, while confiding that the wedding would have to be soon. She needed to marry her Dutch fiancé if she wished to remain in Amsterdam, for although Miep wasn't Jewish and had been living with a Dutch foster family since she was eleven, she had kept her Austrian nationality and was still considered an immigrant, which meant she had to have her passport stamped by the immigration office annually or risk being expelled from the country. Miep had made a vow to never return to Vienna; she was disgusted by Hitler and his antisemitic policies, and she'd made a decision to stay in Amsterdam with her foster family and dear friends, even though much of what was going on around her was growing more and more disturbing all the time. She had even been asked if she would join a women's support group for the Nazis, and had been shocked by some people's ability to overlook the brutality all around them. This refusal, however, led to a withdrawal of her passport by the German consulate and even the previously helpful immigration office could no longer help. The only option was to marry Jan, something they had talked about for a long time. Now they would wed and Miep would be considered a Dutch citizen. On July 16 there was a quiet ceremony, which was small but cheerful. Anne considered every wedding romantic, and she was excited to be included in the planning. She and Miep sat in what had been Otto's office and made lists.

"First the food," Miep suggested.

Anne disagreed with Miep's notions of preparing. There was something more important than food when it came to a wedding celebration. "First the dresses!"

Anne went with her mother to choose her own dress at a shop run by a Jewish seamstress.

"I gave you some extras," the seamstress said. There were pearl buttons and lace sewn to the hem. The dress was so pretty even her mother approved. They walked home with Anne carrying it carefully, for it was a treasure and a privilege to have something so beautiful.

"Don't ruin it," Edith said. "The fabric easily stains."

Anne remembered what her sister had told her. Their mother worried over them. "Thank you for this," she said. "I'll never forget this dress."

Edith looked at her daughter. Anne shone with happiness. She deserved this dress and more. She deserved everything. Edith did her best not to cry. "I'll never forget it either," she said.

✳ ✳ ✳

Miep and Jan were married at city hall, and they were surrounded by those who loved them and wished them well. Some people were loyal no matter what, and their bravery would be more than anyone could have imagined, for Miep and Jan were determined that nothing could affect their friendship with the Franks. Anne attended the marriage with her father, while her mother stayed home with Margot, who wasn't feeling well, and frankly she didn't wish to leave Oma, who was quite ill by now, for too long a time. Anne wore a light coat over her new dress, with a matching hat that was decorated with a ribbon. Everyone felt nervous and elated as they walked to city hall. The following day they all attended a small wedding reception in Pim's office, even Margot, who felt much better, was there, wearing her blue dress. There were platters of food, more than they'd seen for some time. Glasses were lifted to toast to the young couple's happiness. It was so lovely to have something to celebrate, and Miep and Jan were so clearly in love. Anne was the one who presented the gift that the family and their coworkers had found for the newlyweds, a silver tray that Miep adored.

There were glasses of wine and slices of cake, and everyone

told stories about other weddings that made them all laugh. Once upon a time, there was a bride who married the wrong man because she was so vain she wouldn't wear her glasses. Once there was a groom who was so nervous he forgot his suit and had to come to his own wedding in an overcoat and nothing else. After a while, Anne went outside for a breath of air. She watched the green light filtering through the leaves of the trees. She wondered how it felt to be deeply in love, to know you had found what her grandmother called your bashert, your soulmate, the person you were fated to be with no matter what.

Margot had been looking for her sister, who had mysteriously disappeared, and soon followed Anne outside. They both needed a break from the grown-ups' stories of proposals and parties. The sisters stood there together, both thinking about love. They both wondered if they would ever get married, if their weddings would be large affairs or small gatherings, if they would wear white wedding dresses and strands of pearls, if there would still be love in the kind of world they had now.

"Every time I look at a boy, Mama asks me if I'm going to marry him," Anne said.

"It's only that she wants to be certain that we have a future," Margot told her sister.

"I'll choose my own future."

"I will as well," Margot said firmly.

Jews were no longer allowed to be on rowing teams, and the girls on Margot's team who weren't Jewish refused to accept their coach when their teammates were barred from the sport. Ever since then, Margot had seemed different, and now Anne was surprised by how sure of herself her sister sounded. She was usually so eager to please their parents.

"Do you have something in mind?" Anne asked, for she couldn't imagine that Margot would ever dare to rebel.

"I might want to go to Jerusalem." Margot gave her sister a look. "That's where my future is. But do not tell Mama."

They both knew their mother would not approve. Jerusalem was a world away, too far, too hot.

"I want to be a children's nurse or a midwife," Margot told her sister.

"You do?" It was as if Anne didn't know her sister at all. They were two strangers looking up at the trees with secrets they'd never told to anyone or had even spoken aloud. They could see the wedding party through the window. Miep looked so happy and she so deserved every happiness. Maybe some things were fair in this world. Maybe good people didn't have everything taken from them. The girls stood closer to each other in the pale green light.

"I want to bring life into the world," Margot said. "One for every life they've taken away from us."

The Nazis wanted to rid the world of their people, and Margot wanted the opposite. Bringing new life into the world would be a daily miracle.

"You want to make something out of nothing," Anne said. That was the way she felt when she invented her own stories.

Now it was Margot's turn to be surprised. "Exactly."

If these sisters ever knew each other it was now, at this moment, standing beneath the trees, hiding from the grown-ups and from the rest of the world, doing their best to have faith in the future, wishing that this day wouldn't end, grateful for a few hours that focused on love. Red roses were growing nearby, planted outside a factory building. Anne realized how important it was to have courage in a world where hope was difficult to hold on to. People were sleeping in closets. They were escaping into boats that were barely seaworthy.

"Let's make a wish," Anne said. "Together."

Margot laughed. "Aren't we too old for that?"

They would never be too old, Anne declared, so they went ahead and wished. "Come with me," Anne told her sister, and they went down a little, worn path. They held their hands on the bark of the nearest elm tree. "And we can never tell anyone. That way it will come true."

One day they would meet in a garden in Jerusalem surrounded by olive and cypress trees. They would eat figs and honey. They would sit side by side, grown women who had married for love, who didn't quarrel with their husbands just to make them feel bad. One day they would meet in California, where honeysuckle and morning glories flourished almost all year round and the sunshine was always bright. Later, they would forget how close they'd been on the day of Miep's wedding, they wouldn't remember that they had held hands there by the warehouse, how the green leaves fell down all around them. There was the bride just on the other side of the glass, as the grown-ups toasted to the future and the sisters imagined the gardens where they would meet one day.

* * *

That summer the government announced that Jewish children would be forced to go to separate schools. Children all over the city were in shock, bewildered at the way their lives were disrupted as they were separated from the teachers and friends they were so attached to. No matter where in the city they lived, they would all be sent to Jewish schools; they would no longer be allowed to attend any of the public or private schools that Christians attended. Parents of Jewish students at the Montessori school had been notified by letter, and now children were taken out of their classrooms and told of the change that would soon happen. There were tears on the part of both the teachers and students. Anne loved the Montessori school and felt as if she were being sent into exile.

Ninety-one Jewish children would be separated from

their non-Jewish friends and associates. Anne had many friends at school but now she wondered if the ones who weren't Jews would talk to her when they ran into each other. She'd heard of Christian students walking right past people they'd grown up with and had known all their lives without a glance, as if they were complete strangers. By September, new laws had been announced that forbade Jews to go to public places. There were signs everywhere. VOOR JODEN VERBODEN. "Forbidden for Jews." The Netherlands was being divided by the Nazis' beliefs about race, exactly as it had happened in every country the Nazis had controlled. There was a *before* and an *after* and the door to what had once been had closed.

In September, before classes began, Otto decided to bring Anne on a trip to cheer her up, for she was so worried about her grandmother that sometimes she refused to leave the house. They would be going to a hotel near two rivers where there were parks and trails where they could walk freely. Oma could not travel or be left behind, and so Otto had decided it would be just the two of them. Anne was glad to have the time alone with her father. Anne and her father had more to talk about than anyone else in the family because they were readers. It was true, Anne loved him most. His kindness, his love of books, those times when she could tell he was thinking that she was special. She could tell from the way he looked at her, from the way he nodded, from the way he said, "Anne, with a book you will never be alone." And that was how she knew he sometimes felt as she did and that he understood that even when you were surrounded by people, sitting at the dinner table with your family or celebrating a holiday, it was possible to feel as if you were alone, and that when you felt that way, you could open a book and turn the page and feel known by someone you had never even met.

On the train, Pim told Anne stories he had learned during his summer at Heidelberg University, studying with the greatest German scholars of mythology. Stories were something they had always shared, and Anne was always happy to listen, even when she knew the story by heart. First, there was the legend of Icarus, who flew too close to the sun, ignoring his father's warnings as he tried to escape the labyrinth where they were held captive. Then Pim spoke of Pandora, who had dared to open the jar that contained all the evils in the world, setting them free to plague humankind.

Best of all was the tale of Persephone, a beautiful young woman who was kidnapped by Hades, king of the underworld, to be his queen. When he saw Persephone picking a flower, he fell madly in love with her and took her down to the land where only the dead could go. But her mother, Demeter, goddess of the harvest, refused to give up her daughter. Demeter's grief was so huge, all the world stopped growing, and misery and famine resulted. At last, when the world was devastated, Persephone was allowed by her husband to leave the underworld for half the year, the half when there is spring and summer, seasons filled with light and joy. Who wouldn't want a mother who would do anything to bring you back from the underworld? Who would make any bargain and turn the world into dark, cold winter until you were returned to her, even if it was for only half the year? A mother who didn't look at you as if you were a disappointment and quietly give up on you because you thought you were something you weren't, because you just weren't special enough for her to see who you were?

Looking out at the flat fields they passed, it felt as though nothing had changed out in the countryside since the Germans had arrived over a year earlier. There were thatched shelters for goats and low wooden cow barns. If you looked straight ahead, if you didn't think of the arrests and violence in the city, if you forgot all the laws only Jews had to obey, you could almost think that the world was the same. There were still farmers and stacks of hay and small houses with windows high under the eaves. The grass was already turning yellow. They were taking the train out to a small hotel called Groot Warnsborn, a place of peace and quiet. It was a relief to be out of the city, where the changes had been felt more and more. In the past few weeks, many of those who were speaking up had been arrested. It had happened in their own safe neighborhood late at night, when gatherings of Jews were broken up.

People were being watched and followed and arrested. Anne's parents said that children didn't need to know details, but Anne had heard the rumors about Jews in Poland and Germany who had been sent away. She'd heard that Jews were blamed for every disease and disaster that occurred; people said they secretly murdered Christian children, that they couldn't be trusted and weren't truly human. Many feared the Netherlands would be turned inside out with hatred for the Jews, following what had happened in Germany and Austria and Poland. But now, for a few days, out here in the country, Anne could focus on books and nature, as if nothing had changed, even though she saw the black moth every time darkness fell. It followed her up the stairs into her rented room, then disappeared from sight. She told herself it was a figment of her imagination, made up of shadows and fear, but why then could she hear its wings flutter, why was it in the corner of every room?

Anne had a small bag packed. Inside were some clean clothes and pajamas and several books. When they got to the hotel, she decided she would read the novel about a circle of Dutch friends as she curled up on a wooden lawn chair in the garden of the hotel. The girls in the novel were carefree and seemed to have no worries; one was named Kitty. If Kitty was her pen pal, Anne would have written her a letter that described how beautiful the countryside was.

Dear Kitty, we are in a fairyland. The whole world seems so far away. If only we could stay here. If only no one could find us. We would vanish into a world of happiness.

✳ ✳ ✳

They had lunch in the dining room, at a table near the window. There were pom sandwiches, made of roasted chicken and lemon and spices, a Creole-Jewish dish Jews had favored since the 17th century, that Anne and her father hadn't had for some time. The sky was gray but they decided to take advantage of being in the country and went outside as soon as the lunch hour was over, bringing along their books and a cup of strongly brewed tea for Pim.

There was a stream nearby and storks had made nests in the low branches of the trees. But the birds had disappeared, already migrating to the savannas of Africa in expectation of the winter to come. The skies were oddly absent of birds even out here in the countryside, just as they had been in Amsterdam. *Fly away, fly away,* Anne always called to the magpies in the city, for they sat shivering in the trees when all the other birds had gone off to Morocco and Spain to spend the winters in sunlight. The weather was still warm here in the countryside early in the day, but Anne felt chilled late in the afternoon, and she wore a sweater that had been a birthday present in June. It was already too small for her, but she didn't care. In the past, she couldn't wait to grow up, it had always been that way, even though her grandmother had always told her not to hurry getting older. But she couldn't wait till her next birthday. Once she was thirteen, things would be better. She would practically be a grown woman, able to make her own decisions and choose her own path in life.

Pim was in the chair beside Anne's, reading Dickens's *Great Expectations*. Every once in a while, he had tears in his eyes, moved by the extraordinary writing. "Dickens is so right about the world," he explained when he noticed Anne staring, curious about his deep reaction to the book. "He writes about the triumph of good over evil."

"Do you believe that always happens?" Anne asked her father. She knew that it wasn't only the book that made him cry.

Pim placed the novel onto his lap and gazed up through

the trees. The leaves were yellow and the branches were black. While they had been staying at the hotel, new regulations had gone into effect and Pim didn't want to confess his true feelings. He had believed in the ultimate power of good once upon a time, but now he wasn't so sure. He used to believe that the world was fair. He'd been a dreamer, and what was wrong with that, he always said. You had to have dreams before you could make them come true. Yet now he felt defeated. He felt as if he had made a terrible mistake. He should have sent his daughters to England. Even if they had been separated, the girls would have been safer.

He had thought of good and evil as concepts before, but now they felt as real as a stone or a book, as real as a scorpion or a leaf. Good and evil breathed as if they were human; they walked down the streets and slipped under the door, they held you in an embrace or grabbed you by the throat, they comforted you or tore you apart. It was a matter of time before Jews could no longer own businesses, and Otto was planning to sign his business over to his partners, Kleiman and Kugler, and Miep's husband, Jan Gies, a young man they trusted, had become a board member.

Pim knew that Anne would be able to tell if he lied to her, for he was not a liar by nature, and she knew him so well. And so he merely shook his head. He had always tried his best to protect her from the worst of his fears. But on this day, he was truthful, perhaps because Anne seemed so very grown up as they sat there together. The world was changing so fast, and he no longer felt it was possible to protect her from his fears.

"I'm not sure," Pim admitted.

"I am." Anne sounded quite certain of herself. "Good triumphs." This is what she told herself every morning and every night. It's what she made herself believe every time she saw the shadow of the moth in the corners of her room. "I'm absolutely sure of it," she said, more to herself than to her father.

Pim hugged her, proud that his daughter was a strong person. "You're right, of course," he said, but his voice sounded shaky. He was becoming a different man. Someone who had nightmares instead of dreams. A man who was filled with self-doubt.

Anne excused herself then so that she could be alone. She said she was tired and would head back to her room to take a nap, but instead she walked down the path to the stream, past the tall stalks and reeds that were already turning gold at the edges despite the heat of the day. She had to believe that good won out over evil. Why else would there be clouds and trees and love? She would grow up and she would find true love and she would see California and swim in the ocean. That is what she had always told herself and what she had wished for outside Miep's wedding party, and yet she felt shaky as she walked away from her father. She'd said she was sure, but what if she was wrong? What if the world had been turned inside out? What if the monsters in her dreams were able to break through into her waking life?

She went through an iron gate at the edge of the garden, then traipsed through the tall grass, all the while thinking of Persephone, who'd been drawn underground and captured by the king of the underworld. How far away it must have felt to have been there, how very dark and lonely. It was her mother's love that had saved her, when Demeter refused to lose her daughter to the darkness and brought her back to the world above each spring. Anne wondered if her mother would ever embark on such a brave journey to rescue her. Would she scour the whole world until she found her, down in the dark where no human being should ever have to go in an upside-down world where it was easy to be trapped in a place you didn't belong?

It was a relief to be here in the countryside where she felt she was a million miles away from home. The sound of the frogs, the calm surface of the dark slate-blue water, the crickets in the grass. Ever since the night when the bombs had fallen, it had been quiet in Merwedeplein, but it was a quiet that could be broken in seconds by a scream. Here there was only the soft noise of nature. Anne sat in the grass and studied an empty stork nest. The nest had been woven together with great care, but the stork had abandoned it now. Suddenly, Anne spied something blue in the nest. She imagined that she had found a treasure. Perhaps it was a necklace fashioned with a magical blue stone, or it was a secret message from the fairies who lived here, hiding from all human life. Her shoes would get wet if she stepped into the water, but

Anne would set them to dry in the last of the fading sunlight and her father wouldn't know that she had walked through the mucky pool to reach the circle of reeds.

Before she knew it, she was ankle deep. She didn't fall into the underworld as she ventured on. Hades did not come for her on his burning chariot. All the same, Anne's heart was beating fast. It would be so easy to disappear, to be forgotten by everyone who had once known you, to sink down into the netherworld. The water was rushing more quickly than she had expected it to, and for a moment she felt she might be swept away. Still, she made her way into the stream. She reached into the nest perched in the overhanging branch and plucked not a flower, but a blue hair ribbon. It was a simple thing that a thousand girls might have used to tie back their hair. Someone had left it after swimming nearby this past summer. They probably hadn't noticed it was gone until it was too late. Summer was over, and the leaves would turn a wintry brown, but the ribbon was still there and Anne took it as a sign. Blue for happiness, for the good in the world, blue for hope.

She slipped the ribbon into her pocket. It would serve to

remind her to look beyond what other people saw, to see light where there was darkness and remember that even though fall was approaching, in time it would once again be spring.

* * *

In the evenings, Anne and her father had dinner together, then they would play cards. Outside, bats flickered through the darkening sky, and when it grew late, they would go to their rooms and read. The precious hours passed so quickly, and then it was time to go home. In a few short days, they had almost forgotten what awaited them. On the journey back, Pim told Anne some of the stories he'd made up about two girls named Paula, one who was good and the other bad. Anne thought she knew which Paula she was and which one represented Margot, who could do no wrong. She thought the bad Paula was far more interesting, and usually these stories made Anne laugh, but not today.

It was a shock to be back in Amsterdam. Anne had almost forgotten how quickly people walked here, afraid of being stopped and questioned. Anne and her father walked home from the train station holding hands, not speaking.

How could anyone know what they were allowed to say, and what they might be arrested for? Anne was grateful when they arrived home to number 37. Margot was waiting for her sister up in their room, wanting to know every detail of their trip, listening to Anne's report of her time at the hotel as she unpacked her bag, which was mostly filled with books. Margot was too kindhearted to resent the fact that she'd been left at home. It had been Anne who needed to get away and have some fun, and now Margot was simply excited to hear about her sister's travels. Did she wade in the stream? Were there storks nesting this year? Were they served the cookies they'd once had at the hotel, almond-shaped crescents decorated with slivered nuts?

"Everything was different," Anne said softly. They were light-years away from all of those other times they had gone to the country as a family.

"Was it not fun at all?" Margot asked. Her voice was ragged, she had fears of her own, ones she too kept to herself.

"It was," Anne said. She told her sister that she had gone across the stream to the nest, walking on tiptoe as if one wrong step could cause her to drown. She made Margot laugh when she acted out her alleged clumsiness, pretending her feet were stuck in the mud. But when Margot went out to help set the table, and Anne was alone, she wished she was back at the river. She sat on her bed, trying not to cry, for crying would do no good. Her grandmother had told her that, and Oma was right. You thought everything was fine, and then it wasn't. You thought you were on a holiday only to discover that everything had changed while you were gone.

There were no wolves in Amsterdam, not anymore. They had slinked through the marshes and the fields when stones were thrown at them. Whole villages had driven the wolves off with sticks and spears so that they ran as fast as they could. But there were worse things in the world than living in the dark forest. You could hide in the forest, you could sleep on pine needles, you could make your home in a cave where they would never find you. Here in their neighborhood, there were things you wanted to run away from even before you knew what they were. You heard them breathing, you saw them in the dark; they were the goblins who looked like men on the streets, soldiers in uniform. It was these men who had killed the rabbits in the square. They hadn't done so because they were hungry or in need. They did it for sport, they did it because the rabbits stared up at them in the moonlight without even thinking of running, for these creatures had never seen soldiers before. They didn't expect stones and bullets. They had lived in a world of peace for so long that they had forgotten there were far more dangerous things in this world than wolves.

CHAPTER EIGHT

B y the time the school term began in October, some of Anne's non-Jewish friends no longer spoke to her. Many Dutch children had joined the Jeugdstorm, "the Youth Storm," wearing the uniform of the youth who followed the Dutch Nazi party. Anne had seen a girl from her school several times in the neighborhood, the last time when she and Margot were coming home with some vegetables from the market.

"Have nothing to do with her," Margot advised when they spied a gathering of Hitler Youth, Anne's acquaintance among them. "If she talks to you, don't answer."

Anne raised her eyes to the group as they passed on either side of the street.

"What are you looking at, Jew?"

Anne thought it was the voice of her acquaintance, but she quickly looked away, her face burning.

"Good," Margot whispered. "They want to make you angry. Then they'll have reason to attack you."

Anne's eyes felt hot. She wished she could run across the street and shout in her ex-friend's face, but then she felt Margot slip her arm through hers.

"Forget her," Margot said.

"Forgotten," Anne said, turning her back.

"Run away," the girl shouted. "That's what your people do!"

Anne could feel pressure on her arm as her sister tightened her grasp. "Maybe we shouldn't feel so bad about going to the new school," Margot said. There would be only Jews attending, and no one would hate them or call out names as they walked down the hallways. "We'll be fine."

"Will we?" Anne said. She thought of how certain she'd been when she told her father that good always triumphed over evil. Now she wasn't sure at all. Still, on this day, she and

Margot were together and nothing could get between them, nothing could make them run, not as they walked across the square then went up the steps to 37 Merwedeplein.

* * *

It rained on the first day of school, but Margot and Anne rode their bikes, and all that day Anne shivered. She thought her teacher seemed like a gray shadow in a long dress, and although Hanneli was at the same Jewish school as Anne, they were not in the same class. For once in her life, Anne was no longer a chatterbox. She feared she would feel alone and out of place, but the teacher was nicer than Anne had guessed, and she moved Hanneli into the same class. Soon, Anne had the good fortune to make a new friend in Jacqueline van Maarsen, who was at the school because her father was Jewish, even though her mother was Catholic. Jacque was so charming and pretty that Anne immediately declared her to be one of her best friends, and yet she still felt alone. She had been feeling so more and more, ever since the trip to the countryside. When she was by herself, she thought about her dreams. She dreamed she was in a dark place, one she didn't recognize, and there was no one there she knew, and there were monsters guarding all the doors and fires without end burning, and when she cried out, no one knew who she was.

* * *

In winters past, there were bonfires on the canals and the falling snow was something to celebrate, but now there was nothing festive about the cold, gloomy days. This winter, Jews could only watch other people skate. They had to make certain not to stop for too long to watch the skaters or they might draw the attention of the police nearby. It was never good to be noticed by those who wished you were gone and had the power to make it happen. Jews were shadows, walking quickly in their dark clothes, doing their best to remain invisible, but on December 8, the United States officially entered the war, and people had hope again. They looked up to the skies waiting for the bombs to fall, but American soldiers were still far away, and the Germans went on with their plans, arresting more and more Jews, who vanished as if they had never existed.

The sisters prepared a celebratory meal. It was only soup

and some homemade bread that hadn't risen in the pan, but Otto had put away some chocolates and a few oranges.

"To America!" they all cried as they sat around the table.

That night the sisters packed their suitcases, just in case the Americans came to the rescue in the middle of the night. Edith peered into the room and thought her girls very naïve to think they'd be rescued so quickly.

"Things don't always happen so fast," she told them.

The sisters faced her, standing at the ends of their beds.

"Yes, of course," Margot said.

"It happened fast when the Germans bombed us," Anne said. She wanted to be excited about something. She wanted to be woken in the middle of the night, but when they awoke in the morning, nothing had changed in their city. The Americans were still far away. Too far to rescue them in the middle of the night or any other time.

The excitement about the United States entering the war soon had a downside when it came to getting out of the country. The Frank family had been close to freedom, hoping for visas to Cuba, from which they could then head to America, but with the declaration of war, Cuba canceled its visa program. There was no way to leave. Otto stopped writing letters; he set aside his papers and pens. He had already thought of another plan for escape, one he didn't mention to his daughters, one he had hoped he would never have to turn to.

* * *

On her way home from school alone on a cold afternoon, Anne wondered if authors wrote for the same reason she had always read, to escape into another world. As she walked along the river, she began to imagine a story about a grandmother who watched over her granddaughter as if she were a guardian angel. The girl grew up to have a happy life, for even though there was sorrow in the world, her grandmother's love was so strong she could feel it even when her grandmother departed from this world. Anne stopped beside the frozen river, but in her mind, she was inside her story. She was in a garden that was more beautiful than any she'd seen before, with twelve rosebushes, six that were red and six that were white. She imagined that she heard her grandmother's voice. "Come see what has bloomed! Mind the bees!" Without thinking, Anne started to walk onto the ice as if she were entering the garden inside her mind.

"You there!" a German soldier called to her. "What do you think you're doing?"

Anne felt her heart racing. She wasn't inside her story anymore. She didn't know what to do, so she looked down as the soldier approached. She was shaking; she knew she should have paid more attention to what she was doing, but there she was, on the edge of the ice. One more step and she would be breaking the law. He knew who she was, perhaps because of how frightened she looked, or maybe it was her dark glossy hair and her large expressive features, or maybe he merely guessed.

"Jews cannot skate," the soldier said.

Anne had no choice but to talk, even though her voice broke as she did. "I have no skates. I was only looking at a fish."

It was a stupid thing to say, for the fish were all beneath the ice, and the solider made a face, not understanding her meaning. "To steal it?"

"No." She fumbled for words, which was not at all like

her. "I just wanted to see it. It was pretty." Without thinking, she had begun speaking German.

The soldier narrowed his eyes. He was likely not more than eighteen or nineteen, but he seemed older. "You're not Dutch?"

Anne lifted her eyes to him. She was nothing special. She never had been. It had been a mistake to imagine that she was, a foolish desire that would only cause trouble. She should have been the quiet girl who followed the rules. She should have done as she was told.

"I have to go home," she said, speaking in Dutch. Her mother was right. It wasn't safe anywhere in the city.

When Margot noticed that Anne wasn't home, she went looking for her without mentioning what she was doing to her mother, who would only be upset and tell her not to go. Margot followed the route she knew her sister took each day. From a distance, Anne looked like a child standing there with the soldier. Margot walked faster, so fast she was almost running. When she reached her sister, she took Anne's arm. "She doesn't think straight," Margot said to the soldier, pointing to her head, indicating that something was wrong with Anne.

The soldier nodded and before he could say anything, Margot seized Anne's hand and led her away. The girls fled in shame, as if they were criminals.

"There's nothing wrong with me," Anne huffed, insulted and confused, but still terrified by the look on the soldier's face. "I'm perfectly fine."

"Hush. Don't say another word." Margot gave her sister a sidelong look and saw that she was shaking. "Are you all right?"

Anne's heart was beating so hard against her chest that she thought it might fly out of her mouth like a bird. She wondered if fear did that, if it made you lose your heart, if it left you empty inside. "I'm fine," she told her sister. Her voice was breaking, so she looked away.

"Of course you are," Margot said to soothe her. "It's the soldier who isn't fine. You have to be more careful."

"I started talking about fish," Anne said, incredulous at what she had told the soldier, upset by her own foolishness, but then Margot laughed and so did she. "I thought it was a neutral topic."

Margot shook her head. "It's not. I'm sure Jews are forbidden to fish."

"Jews are forbidden to breathe," Anne said.

"That's next." Margot's expression was bitter, which wasn't like Margot at all. Or at least it hadn't been in their old lives.

"There is no neutral topic," Anne realized. "Is there?"

They looked at each other and then Margot said, "Maybe we should go home together from now on."

They had nothing in common except for the fact that they were sisters, but now that seemed to be everything. So that is exactly what they did, and even though they didn't always talk, even though there were days when they didn't say a word, they both felt much better knowing they'd be together.

* * *

Anne's new school friend Jacqueline sometimes invited her to stay over. Jacque's apartment was large and more peaceful than the Franks' house. Her family didn't have to take in a boarder as the Franks did in order to afford the rent on their own apartment. The man living on the top floor of Anne's house was Mr. Wronker, a difficult man in his thirties who helped them pay the rent and called out a greeting every time Anne passed him by. If she had to say hello to him one more time, she thought she would snap and say something rude. All the same, one January night Anne wasn't certain if going to Jacque's was the right thing to do. Oma's condition had grown worse each day. She would no longer eat, not even soup. She could barely rise up from her bed.

"I probably shouldn't go overnight," Anne said to her grandmother. She had packed a small bag, but she was still uncertain. If they didn't have a boarder living on the top floor, Oma would have had her own room. She wouldn't have had to sleep in the dining room with so little privacy that they could all hear her pained coughing at night.

"Go and have fun with your friend," Oma insisted. "Life is for the living."

"You're living," Anne reminded her grandmother.

Oma smiled, kissed her, and waved her hands. She thought about walking through the forests in Germany, she thought about falling in love on a night filled with stars, she thought about her young granddaughter, who had always been so special to her. "I've already lived," Oma said. "Now it's your turn."

It was January 28 and cold enough so that Anne wore two sweaters and a coat and a scarf, along with a hat and mittens and boots. It was so quiet in the Van Maarsens' apartment that Anne could usually sleep the whole night through when she was a visitor there, but on this night she had a dream that her grandmother was falling. The ground had opened and there was the underworld right below the wooden floor. In the morning, Anne had an empty feeling in the pit of her stomach. She really couldn't listen to anything Jacque had to say, and perhaps she was rude. She skipped breakfast even though she was offered a pancake; she packed up and left right away. She ran all the way home, dodging between the parked cars. There were no birds this morning, no children, nothing at all. She realized that she hadn't seen her magpie for weeks, and she took this to be a bad sign. He had been trapped in winter, in days that grew colder, condemned to a world of ice.

As soon as Anne opened the door to 37 Merwedeplein, she knew that something was wrong. She knew from the quiet and from the look on her mother's face. She knew the way she had known that one day her magpie wouldn't return. Her grandmother was gone.

"There was nothing we could do," Anne's mother said. "It was peaceful at the end. That matters."

It didn't matter to Anne. All she knew was that she would never see her grandmother again. She went into the bathroom and latched the door and stood there crying with her back against the door, stunned by grief. She was burning up and freezing at the very same time. She was in a place that was so lonely she didn't know how she would survive. This was what it felt like when you lost someone, when they vanished as if they had never been there. Anne refused to open the door when Edith knocked and pleaded with her to come out.

Perhaps Anne was punishing herself when she sat down on the cold floor. She felt responsible for not being at home on the night when her grandmother had left this world. But when she thought about their last conversation, she wondered if her Oma had told her to go spend the night with her friend in order to protect her from seeing death there in their own dining room. *Life is for the living*, she had told Anne, and then she had kissed her goodbye. It had felt like a true goodbye and Anne had stopped for a moment before she left the room.

Maybe I'll stay, she had said, but her grandmother had waved her toward the door. *Go and don't feel guilty*, her grandmother had called. Oma had reminded Anne that she was alive and young and needed to have faith in the world around her. She reminded her that no matter what happened, no matter how difficult life became, Anne would always know she had been loved.

That winter seemed to last forever. There would be other terrible winters in the years to come and the Netherlands would suffer a terrible famine they would call the Hunger Winter, for the Germans would blockade food and nearly twenty thousand Dutch citizens would die. But now was the winter of fear of the future. Would the Americans save them, or would they all be sent away to camps?

Anne lost weight and grew pale. She didn't want to eat and merely pushed her food around her plate. She refused to sit in the dining room even though Oma's bed had been stored in a closet and the linens and blankets had been washed and put away. The room seemed all wrong without Oma in it. Anne wished she could run away and live with the wolves in the forest. She'd heard that some brave people her age were doing just that, camping in the woods, sleeping in the trees as if they were birds, eating berries that had frozen on the bushes, using moss to make fires so they wouldn't freeze to death.

Edith didn't know that Anne was up at all hours until she heard sudden movements in the kitchen one night, a skittering sound that made her worry that rats had gotten into the house, for they were everywhere in the neighborhood. They too were starving, searching through mounds of garbage, trying to get inside houses so they would stay warm.

Edith pulled on a bathrobe and came into the room with a broom in her hand. "Anne!" she said, surprised when she saw her daughter there. "What do you have to say for yourself?"

Anne had been known for her jokes and now all she could think to do was answer her mother with a joke. "What can't you eat at dinner?" Anne said. She went on even when Edith gave her a narrow look. "Breakfast and lunch," Anne told her.

Once Edith laughed, Anne felt a wash of relief. "Go back to bed," Edith told her. "Eating at night can cause nightmares."

But even as she spoke, Edith knew such rules no longer applied in the world that they lived in. There were nightmares all the time now, night and day, no matter the hour. *Eat when you have food. Eat whenever you can, for there may come a day when there is nothing in the pantry and we have to go out and dig in our neighbors' frozen gardens.*

"But if you're hungry, then you're hungry," Edith granted, changing her tune. "Have what you want."

They sat down together at the table, and Anne finished the leftover dinner, a bowl of vegetables and some bulgur wheat. If this had been another time, Edith would have thrown the stew away days ago. Now, it seemed good enough, it would have to be, since they had to stretch their meals to last. *What were people having for supper in California?* Anne wondered as she finished her leftovers. *Pancakes and champagne and chocolate cake? What were the children hiding in the woods having? Roots and leaves and a tea made from the bark of trees?*

When Anne was done with dinner, Edith took the bowl

and rinsed it at the sink. Anne rose to go, but her mother said, "Wait."

Now she will tell me more of what I've done wrong, Anne thought, for she always expected her mother to be critical, but instead, Edith reached under the sink and took out a small tin box. Inside were the earrings and gold necklace Oma had given her on her eighteenth birthday that Anne had seen her hiding soon after the bombs had fallen.

Edith held out the necklace. "For you," she said.

Anne took a step back. There was something wrong in this. She was too young for such a special gift. She was the little sister, the one who never pleased her mother, the one who wasn't so special after all. "You don't have to give it to me," she stammered.

"Of course I don't have to," her mother told her. "I want to."

"I can't wear it anyway." She'd heard that Germans tore the jewelry off Jewish women in the street, grabbing the rings from their fingers.

"You don't have to wear it outside, you can keep it where it is, and you'll know it's yours," Edith said. "Even if it's hidden."

Anne lifted her eyes to her mother's. It was then that she

saw something she'd never expected. She saw that her mother would do anything for her, that she would search the world over for her if Anne fell into the underworld; she would make the trees turn brown and shake them with all her might until they lost their leaves, she would scour the whole world until she found her daughter. They didn't get along, but it wasn't because they were opposites, rather because they were so alike.

Anne wondered if her mother was giving her the necklace because there might not be time to do so if she waited until Anne was eighteen. She couldn't bear to think this might be true, and so Anne handed the necklace back. "Please, Mama, give it to me on my eighteenth birthday just the way Oma gave it to you."

"Are you sure?" The future was something Edith had looked forward to, and she wanted the same for her daughters, but she feared that it wouldn't come to pass.

"I'm sure I want to wait," Anne told her mother.

Edith nodded and returned the necklace to its hiding place.

It was dark outside, and the moon was a silver disc. It was as if they were the only two people in the world. Anne had resented her mother in the past, and she would be annoyed with her again, but now they understood each other, at least for a little while.

Edith nodded. "I'll wait until you're eighteen," she said. "It will be our secret."

Once upon a time, there was a girl who realized that her mother loved her. It happened suddenly, it happened in the kitchen, when it was so late the sun would soon be rising. From now on she would try to remember that. When she was angry and disappointed in Edith, when she felt they had nothing in common, she would do her best to recall this night when her mother was hiding the necklace back beneath the sink. Five years would pass in no time, and then Anne would be eighteen. Anne made a wish that on that day she would be in California and her mother would come to visit her and they would sit under a palm tree in a place where the sky was always blue, and her mother would give Anne the gold necklace and they would both agree that it had been best to wait and that the future was right here and that they hadn't lost everything after all.

CHAPTER NINE

Margot turned sixteen on February 16. It was a Monday, and Edith and Otto had decided to celebrate despite the darkening mood in the city and the despair they all felt. Margot's gift was a book she had wanted, *Camera Obscura*; there were cards, and Otto wrote the traditional birthday poem, which he recited after cake was served. They all applauded, and the candles were blown out quickly so that they would not be wasted.

"How does it feel to be sixteen?" Anne asked her sister.

Margot laughed. "I feel exactly the same as I did yesterday. I've always been the same."

Anne felt herself flush with resentment because it was true. Her sister had been a perfect baby and a perfect child and now was on the verge of becoming a perfect woman.

Then Margot surprised her when she suddenly turned away, distraught.

"This may be as old as I ever get to be," Margot said. She went into the small toilet room, then she locked the door.

"Margot," Anne whispered.

"Go away," Margot responded. She didn't even sound like herself. She sounded like someone who was afraid of the future. No matter how good she was, no matter how perfect, she couldn't set things right.

All that day, Anne thought about her sister, who was beautiful and kind and who had cried on her birthday. They had never been really close; they'd been too different for that, but something between them had changed. It wasn't all the time, most days they ignored each other. But there was the day when Anne had stepped onto the ice in front of the soldier and the afternoon when they'd stood beneath the elm trees after Miep's wedding. Anne remembered those times, and she no longer thought her sister was too perfect to ever fall apart. She went into the kitchen, where her mother was washing up.

It was a miracle Edith had managed to make a birthday

cake when so few ingredients were available at the market. She'd been hoarding things in order to bake the cake—flour and butter and a bit of chocolate. Instead of bread, they'd been having matzoh, which requires no eggs, sugar, or salt, and is the bread of poverty and of travelers. There was no matzoh on this day, only delights. Licorice and tapioca pudding and the sweet doughnuts called sufganiyot they usually ate to celebrate Hanukkah.

Edith was wearing an apron patterned with red roses. As she rinsed the dishes in the sink, she was remembering cooking with her mother in Germany when she was a girl. She used to roll out the dough for pies and tarts. The flour would rise into the air like snow and they would laugh and not think of anything other than the pie they were making, the blackberries they had picked, the cream they would whip for a topping. Life was simple then and it was possible to believe in things, but who could believe in anything now? Anne came to stand beside her mother. She thought of her sister talking to the soldier. She thought of them walking home quickly afterward, arm in arm.

"I've been thinking over your offer," Anne said.

Edith turned from the sink to look at Anne, puzzled. "What offer?"

Anne looked straight ahead. She didn't want to give her emotions away. "Our secret. The necklace."

Edith let the dishes be and stood with her back against the sink. Her younger girl was always a puzzle. "Have you?"

"I think it's more suited for Margot. And I don't think you should wait until she's eighteen."

Edith thought of all the times she had been annoyed with Anne for not being serious enough. She now understood that all those times had meant nothing, and this moment meant everything. Oma had always told Edith to look inside her daughter, but Edith had been too busy with daily life and with the threats all around them. Now she looked and she saw who her daughter was. "Are you sure?" she asked Anne.

Anne nodded. "Extremely sure. I think you should give it to her now."

Eighteen was a year that might never come.

"Why wait," Edith agreed.

That night Anne pretended to be asleep when their mother came into their room. The moon was still bright and the light outside seemed made of silver.

Margot sat up in bed when she realized that Edith was there. "Is everything all right?" she whispered to their mother.

Edith reached for her older daughter and placed her necklace in the palm of her hand. "A special gift," she said. "It belonged to Oma, and then to me. Now it's yours."

Margot threw her arms around her mother. Her face was beaming. "It's so beautiful." She had always loved that necklace.

"You should only wear it inside the house. Just for now. Until things change."

"Of course," Margot said, understanding that if the Germans spied anything that was worth something it would be taken from you. She looped the necklace around her throat, then turned so that her mother could close the clasp. As she did so, Edith looked over at Anne and she knew she wasn't asleep. She knew a lot of things now that she had looked inside her younger daughter just as Oma had always told her to do. At last, after all this time, she knew how special Anne was.

✳ ✳ ✳

The city that had always been open to people who were persecuted and mistreated was closing the doors to freedom, and those who resisted, those who met to plan how to rescue themselves or tried to rescue their neighbors and friends, disappeared and were never seen again. Everyone suspected that a work camp was a place where you were worked to death. Soon, it would be decided that you were worthless the moment you stepped off the train; if you were an old woman or a child or a man who looked weak, you would be sent immediately to the death that was waiting for you.

Some people were going into hiding, some in cellars, some in closets, some in garden sheds. Dozens of families from their neighborhood would find secret places to stow away, and there would be many other teenagers who were Anne's age hidden all over the city. When there was nowhere to run, you had to invent a place, somewhere where you could be hidden until times were better, until the Americans came.

Each day Otto and his partners brought more supplies to the attic at the warehouse. Blankets, sheets, boots, paper and pens, sweaters, cans of food, furniture, books, pots and pans. Pim wished he had sent the children to the cousins who lived in England, he wished they had gone to Switzerland, he wished he could roll back time and look at the world with a clear, cold eye and not be swayed by hope or his insistence that the family must be kept together. He had thought it best not to be torn apart from one another, but how do you know what you cannot know?

At night Anne often told herself the same reassuring message. *Nothing bad will happen.* She whispered it three times as if it were an incantation, a spell to keep away the darkness. Sometimes at night, Margot got into bed with her and Anne could feel her sister's warmth beside her. She had always been too jealous of Margot to really see her, and now she saw that her older sister was afraid. Margot was thinner than she used to be, but she was still beautiful and kindhearted, as she always had been, only now Anne could see inside her. They were completely different and yet they were the same.

"Tell me a story," Margot said.

Anne laughed. Margot was always the one who could fall asleep easily, but now she was the one who wished for a story.

"Really," Margot said. They looked at each other through the dark. "You're so good at it."

Anne nodded. "Once upon a time," she began.

But how could she tell her sister the tragic Greek myths she loved best, the one about the girl who was kidnapped and taken down to the underworld, or the one about the girl who was turned into a spider, or the girl who had opened the jar that had allowed evil into the world? In myths, humans were bent and broken by fate and by the gods. Sometimes they lived and sometimes they died and the world still went on, with or without them.

"Go on," Margot said. Her voice was unexpectedly soft. She thought she had seen a black moth fluttering out in the hall, trying to get underneath their door, and the sight had shaken her. Maybe it was only her imagination, or maybe it was more. Maybe she was beginning to see what was out there. "Tell me a story."

Anne leaned in closer so that their foreheads were touching. "Once upon a time, there were two sisters who were so brave, even the wolves in the woods ran away from them."

"The wolves were afraid of them?" Margot said in disbelief. "Impossible."

"The sisters outsmarted them."

The girls were whispering now. The quiet outside in the city was alarming because you knew there could be a round of gunfire at any moment. Falsified documents allowed members of the Resistance to slip through Dutch life and do what they could to help people escape from the Netherlands. When they were caught they were shot, or sent away to a place that was worse than the underworld that Persephone had known, a place from which no one ever returned, not for spring or for summer, never again. The girls in Anne's story were searching for a place where they could be safe.

"What happened then?" Margot asked.

"And then it snowed and everything turned white and the wolves ran away to hide and the two sisters made their way through the forest."

When Anne closed her eyes, she could see the place she was inventing; it was somewhere far away, somewhere where no one could hurt them, a world of her own making, one she had invented for the two sisters, where the men who were evil were always defeated; they fell into rivers or were buried in the ground. Good people triumphed because they were supposed to. Wolves never attacked two girls who knew how to run away and hide.

"Were they going to California?" Margot asked.

"No, not California." She was done with thinking about Hollywood and the Pacific Ocean. All she wanted was a forest where no one could find them. She wanted a bed of reeds, a coat of thorns, a sword in case the monsters arrived at the darkest hour of the night.

Margot's face was so pale she looked as if she had bathed in moonlight.

"It was a secret place," Anne went on. "It was a place only they could find. They had to walk all night, and they were covered with snow, but then they saw the house at the edge of the forest. A fire was lit in the fireplace and there was food set out on the table. There were two cakes and two pans of noodles and two cups of hot cocoa. There was a door with a thousand locks and when they were turned the house became invisible. All anyone could see were the roses in the garden that grew up through the snow."

They could both hear the black moth slipping under the door now.

"Once upon a time," Anne whispered. "We were there."

Maybe they could sleep for a hundred years, the way girls did in fairy tales.

Their mother opened the door and peeked in and thought they were both sleeping. All the lights in the house had been turned off. When the door closed, the girls opened their eyes.

A story could do many things; it could make you see the beauty in the world, it could give you hope when there was none, but in the end a story was only a story. It was not a black moth Anne had been seeing in the corners. It was evil. It was already in their room. The sisters had imagined how they might escape into the forest to a place so deep in the woods they would never be found. They had no idea that at the end of January, the Final Solution had been drawn up at a secret meeting in a suburb of Berlin, where high Nazi officials planned the killing of the eleven million Jews of Europe and beyond, a genocide of such enormous proportions it would destroy an entire race. Anne and Margot had heard the moths at the window, but they still had faith in the future. They still held hands when they said good night. *Sleep well*, they said, *sleep until the morning light, until the future arrives, until we are anywhere but here.*

What We Lost

Our houses, our savings, our businesses were all taken away. We could own nothing, only our personal property, clothes and furniture, spoons and forks.

We could not enter museums or libraries, not restaurants, not the theaters or the zoo, or any public buildings, even markets that weren't meant specifically for Jews. Dogs were allowed to sit on park benches, but we were not. We were banned from cinemas and cafés. By the last day of May we could no longer use swimming pools, parks, spas, or hotels. We could no longer own radios. There were signs we didn't want to read. They all said the same thing. Jews not allowed.

We could not go to their schools. Dutch children dressed in Nazi uniforms and marched through the streets. We gave our babies away so that they might have a chance to live.

They came for us at any time. A knock on the door was all it took. There weren't enough locks in the world to keep us safe. They said we were the problem, they said they had a solution, and that's when we knew the time had come.

PART FIVE

Hour of Darkness, Hour of Light
Amsterdam, February 1942—July 1942

The star that had been sewn onto her coat burned through her as if the fabric had been spun from pure hatred. Every stitch pierced through her as if it were a thorn. At night, she looked up at the sky and saw that there were still millions of stars right above her, all burning bright, but people on the street didn't notice them. They only saw the one that had fallen. The one sewn to her coat with black thread.

The star that she wore was the only one that mattered now.

CHAPTER TEN

There was less and less food now that the Germans were commandeering most of the fruits and vegetables that were delivered from farms in the countryside. The Jewish market had only the items that no one else wanted, and the Germans had outlawed kosher meat. Battered squash, bruised apples, cabbage that was past being green and had white, translucent leaves. There were more and more rats all the time. Anne and her mother and sister pretended not to see them when they went shopping. You had to pretend some things in order to remain human, you had to try your best to be the person you were before this all began. They imagined the rats were only shadows in the corners. They told themselves this was the market they used to go to, the one that Jews were now forbidden to enter.

"We'll get what we can and make the best of it."

Edith said this every time they went shopping, as if those words were a magical incantation that would make their journey to the market more successful.

"Yes, of course," Margot agreed. "We can make soup."

They looked at one another and said no more. Soup was what they always made to get them through the week. It was a mystery dish that could last a very long time; add water and salt and pepper and there was more of it every day.

Anne was watching the corners of the alley where the market was set up. It was a makeshift place with torn awnings. She had begun to see grief everywhere, even when she didn't want to, even when she closed her eyes. There was so little to buy and so little to sell. A small rat, too frightened to move, sat in a corner, not a shadow at all. The black moths Anne always thought she saw were everywhere. She might be imagining them, but other people seemed to startle when they flitted by.

"Will you get the potatoes?" Edith said to Anne. "As few rotten spots as possible," she added, because the last time, Anne hadn't paid enough attention.

Was this the way the world was supposed to be? Anne believed in faith and loyalty, she believed that people got what they deserved, but who deserved what was happening now? People were shoving to get closer to the vegetable bins. There were carrots today that were worth quarreling over. Two women were discussing who had been there first in loud voices until it wasn't a discussion at all, and one pushed the other. Anne wished she could disappear. She wished she could close her eyes and that when she opened them again she'd be in another country. She'd be so far away no one could find her. She could not bear to think life would be no more than it was. Fighting for vegetables. Not looking at rats. She kept her head tilted so no one would know how lost she felt inside.

"Can you pay attention to me when I speak?" Edith said to Anne.

"There's something in my eye," Anne told her mother. It wasn't exactly the truth, but it could have been.

"Let me see."

Edith came toward her and took Anne's chin in her hand so that she could look into her daughter's eyes. She'd once thought it was possible to change your fate; even if you were in an unhappy marriage, you could do your best and bring happiness into each day in some small way. Now she didn't know what she believed anymore. "Are you crying?" Edith asked, surprised when she saw the tears in Anne's eyes. Her brave daughter who did as she pleased and thought she was special. What had made her cry? They were merely buying vegetables.

"No," Anne was quick to answer as she wrenched away. "I'm not." She couldn't wait to be thirteen. She couldn't wait for the time when people stopped questioning her as if she were a foolish child.

"You look like you are," Edith said. "What's wrong now?"

It was the market that had made her feel like crying, not so much the women arguing over vegetables, but another woman Anne had spied as she searched through the nearly empty bins. This woman had been so intent on finding some potatoes that she had left her baby on the cobblestones, and it had begun to wail.

"Anne has dust in her eye," Margot said, rescuing Anne from her mother's interrogation. Anne threw her sister a grateful look. "The tears wash out the dust," Margot explained.

"Fine." Edith nodded. "Let's see what we can find that's half-decent before it's all gone." She looked straight at Anne. "Crying won't help us now."

"Thank you," Anne said to Margot when it was just the two of them standing side by side waiting for their mother to give the grocer their food coupons. Anne kept her voice low.

Margot smiled and shrugged. "For what?"

"For the lie."

They both laughed then. It was lovely when they felt like confidantes, and it didn't happen very often, or at least it hadn't until recently.

"It was just a little white lie. I know she means well," Margot whispered.

"Does she?" Anne watched her mother pack the vegetables into a cloth shopping bag.

"Of course she does," Margot said. "People are always hardest on their favorite."

Anne felt her face grow hot with shame. "I am not her favorite."

Margot shrugged. "You're the one she's always talking about. You're the one she worries over."

"Because I don't behave. She worries because I think too highly of myself, and I don't get good grades at school."

Margot shook her head. "It's because you're the baby."

Anne felt herself flush. "I am not."

"Well, you were, and you were sick so often when you were little. She worried then, and she still does."

Anne had always been certain that Margot was their mother's favorite; why wouldn't she be? Anne was difficult, her mother said so all the time, and she knew that she never went out of her way to be nice to her mother and Margot always did. Behaving kindly came naturally to Margot. But as they walked home the oddest thing happened. Edith linked her arm through Anne's. It was unusual for her to do so, and Anne looked at her mother, confused.

"I don't want you to stumble if you can't see because of the dust in your eye," Edith said.

"I'm fine," Anne said, even though her throat felt hot and her eyes did as well.

"Just in case," her mother told her.

On another day, Anne might have pulled away, but on this day, Anne remained arm in arm with her mother. She thought of the underworld, and what would have happened if Demeter had never rescued her daughter. There would be no spring or summer, no trees, no leaves, no birds, no life.

They would spend the rest of the afternoon peeling potatoes and chopping onions, and that would be a good excuse to cry. Onions caused tears and there would be no need for her to explain herself. The same would be true for her mother and sister. Margot took her other arm, and Anne felt fortunate to be between them. They walked home quickly, even though the sky was bright. *Mother*, she thought, *what will happen to us? We should run away or we'll be trapped like the magpies. We will never be able to leave if we wait too long.*

As if Edith could read her daughter's thoughts, she tightened her hand on Anne's arm and said, "All we have to think about is the soup."

This wasn't true, but Anne nodded. She accepted that that was what they would do. By now, she knew the recipe by heart. *Potatoes, water, salt, pepper, onions, carrots, if you had them. Cook it longer than you think you should, simmer the broth until it seems like the soup you used to have, when the world was different, when you took dinner for granted, when you didn't make certain to eat every bite just in case there were no potatoes the next time you went to the market.*

Anne had always scribbled her thoughts on paper; to ensure that no one would read them, she would most often tear up what she had written into tiny pieces, like snowflakes that had been marked with ink. She wrote more all the time, bits of stories. Sometimes she stuffed the pages under her mattress and reread them before she destroyed them. They were her secret. They were what she was made of. The words came to life once they were written down.

Anne made a list of all the things that had disappeared. It had begun slowly and then it wasn't slow at all. It was one thing and then it was everything. That was how the Nazis took over, so that people didn't understand what was happening until their dignity was stripped away and they were no longer considered human. One, two, three and the world had shrunk to nothing.

As time passed, more and more rules were set out, and it would continue. No library books, no sitting in the park, no entrance into public buildings, no swimming pools, no vacations or holidays, no hotels, no Jews teaching in schools and universities, no Jewish business to be owned, no radios. Jews who protested were deported; Jews had to deposit their money into a certain bank, where it was stolen from them; Jews had to register any property, then sell it and give the profits to that same bank; Jews were barred from certain professions; Jews were forbidden from riding in cars; they were not allowed to use streetcars, buses, or trains, and eventually could not own bicycles; they could not row or play hockey or be part of any athletics; Jews could not even sit in their own gardens after eight p.m.

They knew what they were being told. *You are different,*

you are an outsider, you cannot have what we have, not the simplest thing, you are a mouse, a fly, a speck of dust. You are not like the other people walking down the street, you are a shadow, you are no longer human. They have the power and you have none, and because of this they can treat you as if you were nothing more than a moth they had caught in a jar, a jar they shake whenever it pleases them, a jar they can empty onto the fire, a jar they keep you in until you are in flames.

CHAPTER ELEVEN

Before the Germans came, the Franks would have a festive celebration at Purim, which marked Queen Esther's saving her people from being destroyed by their enemies. Families and friends would be invited and large dinners would have been laid out on the table, with dishes of sweets for the children. They would dress up and perform plays, and Anne would always take the part of Esther. It couldn't be the same this year, but Anne decided she wanted something to be better.

"May I tell the story of Purim?" she asked at the end of their dinner.

"Of course," Pim agreed, and so she'd gone off to her room to retrieve what she'd written. "This will make the evening," Pim said when she returned to the table with her notebook.

They all stared at Anne; even her mother waited to clear the table so that Anne could tell the story of Esther, an ordinary girl who saved her people when she pretended not to be a Jew so she could marry a king. When the Jews were in danger, Esther admitted her faith and begged for her people's lives. *Once, in the land of Persia, where we were not free, there was a girl who was not afraid to be herself.*

When she was done, her father called out, "Bravo!" and Margot applauded, her eyes shining. Anne glanced at her mother, nervous. Edith did nothing more than nod before she went into the kitchen, carrying their dinner plates to the sink. Anne could feel a fury rise inside her. Not one kind word, not a single word of praise. Anne rose from the table so that the chair skittered behind her; she felt heat rise into her face as she followed her mother into the kitchen. She could not be silent.

"Is there nothing I can do right?!" she cried.

Edith turned to her daughter. She didn't often share what she felt. Not everyone had such wonderful girls, and people could be jealous just as fates could be cruel. Margot was delightful, a perfect daughter, but Anne had been someone special from the moment she was born. She had howled as if she had all the strength in the world; she had studied everything around her so carefully, it was always as if she could see what others could not. From the very start she had been difficult and different from other children, and Edith had been afraid for her, for the world had little tolerance for such people. She thought she could mold her younger daughter into the person she needed to be in order to survive the harshness she was bound to encounter. It was easier to play by the rules, to not want so much, but on this night, she finally realized that was not who her daughter was.

"Tell me!" Anne said. Her voice was breaking, but she didn't care. Her nights were filled with words from the books she read, and her dreams had been filled with them as well. She had put all of her emotions into telling Esther's story. She had made the story her own.

Edith set down the plate she'd been washing. "Fine. If you want to know, then I'll tell you."

Anne feared what she might hear, but there was no going back. *Tell me even if it hurts me. Tell me the truth.* "Of course I want to know!" she told her mother. "Do you think your thoughts don't matter to me?"

Anne had never realized how much she yearned for her mother's approval. Her mother didn't seem to pay attention to her, but she was paying attention now. Anne didn't sound like a little girl anymore. She was nearly thirteen, the number that could be lucky or unlucky, depending on the circumstances.

They stared at each other and then for the first time Edith told her daughter the truth, holding nothing back. "I think you are a storyteller," she said. "Perhaps you will turn out to be a writer."

Anne carried what her mother had said inside her heart; she carried it everywhere she went because she knew it was true. She'd known it even before her mother had said so.

She would be a writer.

One day in April, Anne's bicycle was stolen sometime between noon and two, in broad daylight, with no one daring to stop the thief. A bicycle was everything, freedom, joy, transportation, and to cheer her, Pim took Anne past the booksellers' market. There were outdoor stalls of volume after volume;

many of the editions were antiques, with gold leaf letters and drawings and maps inside. There used to be many Jewish antiquarians, but they had disappeared, packing up their most precious books, wrapping them in blankets, hiding them in cellars and attics or burying them under lime trees in wooden boxes that would unfortunately rot in time. The Oudemanhuispoort Book Market had been in the same place since the 19th century. There it was possible to find sheet music, postcards, old novels, rare books, maps, poetry. No books by Jewish authors could be sold and Jews were forbidden from selling books there. But for those who knew about it, there was an alleyway where books were still traded at twilight, sold out of cardboard boxes rather than the wooden bureaus and cabinets set up in the market. There was one Jewish bookseller who was called Old Edgar, and Otto Frank went to him when he was looking for novels written by Dickens. He was in need of *A Tale of Two Cities*.

"Who is this?" Old Edgar said when he spied Anne with her father. "Let me guess!" He closed his eyes for a moment, thinking, then opened his eyes and grinned. "You're a professor looking for books about the history of our city."

Anne shook her head. "Not at all. I don't even intend to live here when I get older. I'm going elsewhere."

"A world traveler," the old man said.

"Simply a booklover," Otto said of his daughter, a compliment that caused Anne to flush with pride.

While her father and the bookseller got to chatting, she looked around. She saw Old Edgar's wife sorting through a box of old books in a doorway. The books they had to sell were mostly hidden under blankets that Edgar's wife had knitted. She was wearing a black coat and a blue headscarf and for some reason she made Anne think of the magpie she hadn't seen in such a long time. Perhaps it was because the old woman nodded as if she knew Anne; maybe that was the similarity, they looked inside each other and saw what they shared in common. A dread of this city, the need to keep your deepest thoughts secret, a passion for books.

Otto Frank came to introduce Anne formally. "Anne Frank, please make the acquaintance of Edgar DePina's wife, Madame Clara."

The booksellers were Sephardic Jews whose ancestors had first come to Amsterdam in the 1500s during the Inquisition, when Jews were murdered in every town square in Spain and Portugal. The DePinas had been part of a wealthy banking and shipping family, but the businesses didn't belong to them anymore. The Germans had taken them over and their elegant house had been taken as well, their paintings ripped from the walls, some of them old Dutch masterpieces, one a small work by Rembrandt. Wealthy Sephardic Jews had been especially targeted by the Germans, who wished to take their property and belongings, and now many were homeless; some lived in the stables and cellars of their onetime employees who were kind enough to take them in. Old Edgar and his wife lived in a shed owned by a Dutch friend, and they'd been lucky enough to be able to keep boxes of the books that had once been in their library.

While Otto and Old Edgar discussed which was Dickens's best novel, Anne looked around at the stacks of books beneath the blanket. So often when she read novels she felt as if the characters were her friends, and every now and then, even though she knew she would seem foolish if anyone found out, she wrote to the fictional characters about her life.

"I have a book for you," Madame Clara said as she began to knit without having to look at her stitches.

"Oh, no, thank you," Anne said, certain they couldn't afford it.

"I suspect you tell stories."

"Not really," Anne said, embarrassed.

Madame Clara placed her knitting in her lap and pursed her lips, then rose from her chair and signaled to Anne to follow her farther down the alleyway. Pim was involved in his conversation with the woman's husband, so Anne followed. "We're not coming back after today," Clara said. "We're going into the countryside and leaving everything behind. I would hate to have this book destroyed. The Germans will burn whatever they find." She took an old volume from a pile of books that had been stacked against a brick wall. "Would you burn birds in a cage?" she asked Anne.

"Of course not." Anne thought of the magpie. She thought of the soldiers shooting at whatever they saw, just for fun.

"And yet they burn books. They throw them into metal

trash cans and light a fire and then all the words that had been written fly away."

"What happens to the words then?" Anne asked.

"They're remembered by everyone who ever read them." Madame Clara's bright eyes were trained on Anne. It was dark in the alley and Anne had the urge to run, but she stayed where she was. "I used to have everything," the bookseller's wife said. "Now I just have what I can remember."

Madame Clara handed the volume to Anne. It was a book of Greek and Roman myths and Anne marveled at how beautiful it was, the cover illustrated in black and gold, the inner pages decorated with intricate drawings. Inside was the story that had captivated her more than any other. Persephone's journey to the underworld. She noticed there was the imprint of a rose on the leather-bound cover of the book.

"We can't afford it." Anne reached out to return the book. Her nails were bitten to the quick. She had decided to wear her winter gloves, to hide the fact that there were red rims around each nail.

"You must buy it," Madame Clara said. "Then you'll

remember me along with the words. I'll be gone by tomorrow, just like these stories."

Anne wanted to say to the bookseller's wife, *Take me with you wherever you're going. I'll help you carry the books and we can bury them out in the countryside where they'll be safe and someday a girl my age will dig them up and find them and they will be a treasure she will never forget.* Instead, she said, "Thank you. You're very kind. But I'll have to ask my father."

Anne went to her father with Clara's book. Pim linked an arm around her as he continued to cheerfully argue with Old Edgar about Dickens. When he saw that his daughter had a book in hand, he turned to her, shamed by all he could not give her, the simple things that in the past they hadn't been grateful enough for having. Sweets and sugar, new clothes, bicycles, train tickets, visits with family, safety, books.

"Anne, I'm sorry," Pim began. And then he looked at her and changed his mind. He put down the Dickens volume. "We'll take this one," he said, holding up the book of myths. "Don't tell your mother," he told Anne as he paid for the volume. "It will be a birthday present. I'll save it until June."

"You don't have to," Anne told him. "I'm fine without it. Really."

They looked at each other and laughed because they both knew he would buy the book for her. He had always been the sort of man who believed that books were as important as food when it came to nourishing a person. It might have been the last belief he managed to hold on to, one he refused to give up. He had taught her that the ancient myths grasped best the emotions inside everyone, the fear of being abandoned, of letting evil into the world, of wanting to go so high you would fly too close to the sun. Anne and her father walked home without speaking, which was rare for them. They both knew that if they went looking for the bookseller next week or the week after, the old man would be gone, and his wife would be gone as well, having lost everything she'd once had, the elegant house, the rugs, the paintings, the closet filled with clothes and shoes, the books they had loved.

"Almost home," Pim said as they rounded a corner. He always breathed a sigh of relief when they had come this far without being stopped. Not that they'd done anything wrong, but still, they had books, and books by Jews had been outlawed. They were passing the Blankevoort Bookstore. There in the window was the checked journal Anne so wanted. She always stopped and stared at it, as she did now. She'd already be getting the mythology book; it would be greedy to ask for more. And yet, when she thought of all she could confide to that diary, her heart beat faster. She could tell it everything and not be judged or thought to be foolish.

Her father was watching her with a smile, for in his opinion there was no such thing as too much when it came to books.

"You never know what you'll find on your birthday," he said.

Anne took her father's hand. He spoiled her, she knew, and she was grateful. Thirteen would not be like all her other birthdays. It was something special. It was the door that opened to the rest of her life, the day she'd been waiting for, finally the moment in which she might allow herself to be herself.

* * *

When Anne read, the world opened up. The other world, where good people didn't suffer, where magic was possible, where women who resembled her grandmother could give her the advice she badly needed. Two hours later, she had the sense that no time had passed. She was thinking about skating; she was remembering when they were allowed to do things like that. How Margot would wear a red skirt and a black coat and turn circles on the ice. How she would stand in the middle of the canal, the fish sleeping below her, little slips of silvery light, how she would turn her face to the sky and let snow-flakes fall on her cheeks. She took up a pad and a pen and made a list of beautiful images. She started to cry while she was writing, but it wasn't from sadness, it was from getting something right. The blue snowflakes, more delicate than lace, the cool gray diamond light, light she would never forget.

"Are you sleeping?" Margot asked from her bed. She was paler than she used to be, and her eyes seemed darker, or maybe it was just the pangs of worry about the future that made her gaze so brooding.

Anne turned on her side and raised herself up on one elbow. "I'm dreaming," she said.

Margot laughed her beautiful, soft laugh. "With your eyes open?"

"Exactly. That's the best way. That's the way I can think up a story."

Curious, Margot came to lie beside her sister. She was shivering and so she slipped under the blanket. She didn't tell Anne about the remarks German soldiers sometimes made as she walked by. Terrible things. Things that made it impossible to dream and made her feel that it wasn't safe to be a woman. She had wanted to be sixteen so badly, but that seemed a long time ago.

"Tell me a story," Margot said.

Anne made a face. She didn't like to share her deepest thoughts.

"Just a little one," Margot urged.

Margot closed her eyes and listened. She breathed more and more deeply, and then she fell asleep, her eyelids fluttering. Anne slipped her notebook back under the pillow and watched her sister sleep. It took a long time for Anne to fall asleep and when she did, she dreamed someone had come into their room. Someone had sat beside her and stroked her hair. *Sleep my darling*, the person had said so softly it was almost possible for Anne to think she had imagined those words, but in the morning she remembered. Those were the words her mother had said when she'd come in to say good night.

In May, all Jews older than the age of six were made to wear yellow stars on their clothing. It was to identify them to anyone who passed them by, it was to humiliate them and mark them as different. Jews were instructed how and where the crude stars must be worn. Left side, breast high, visible at all times. They had to stand in line outside the synagogue to pick up the cheap yellow fabric, which they were made to pay for, then cut out and sew on the stars themselves. The Jewish Council the Nazis had installed had suggested they should all be proud to wear the Star of David, the symbol of their faith, and some among them even said the star would protect them from evil, that it was a sign of the Jews' solidarity. But most people were quiet and frightened; they understood that the source of their pride was now being made to humiliate them. *You are not us. We can tell who you are even when you are halfway down the street. We can cross over, call you names, spit if we please.*

Otto Frank told his daughters that in a few months the Americans would arrive. It hadn't happened as quickly as they'd hoped, but eventually the war would be over, and then all the madness around them would be defeated by the peacemakers. He had lost his faith in many things, but he still believed that eventually the Allies would win the war. When that happened, they would tear the stars from their clothing. They would unlock their doors and stand out on the street to applaud their rescuers. But for now, the girls in school never spoke about the stars on their clothing. They acted as if the yellow badges weren't even there. As the weather grew warmer, their mothers unstitched the stars from their children's heavy wool coats and sewed them onto light sweaters. Sometimes Anne pretended a star had drifted down from the sky and had been cut into pieces before it was sewn to her, a light that could not be extinguished no matter how hard anyone might try.

✳ ✳ ✳

One afternoon, Anne was talking with a girl she knew named Wilma alongside the bicycle shed near the Skyscraper on the far side of the square. It was an ordinary day, at least for the times they were in, but wasn't that when unexpected things happened? A tall, lanky boy came from out of nowhere, as if he'd appeared from thin air, and headed straight toward them. Anne was nervous; she no longer trusted strangers, especially not since her run-in with the soldier, but then the boy waved and called out Wilma's name.

"Who is that?" Anne asked.

"My cousin from Germany," Wilma told her. "Be careful. Everyone falls in love with him."

"I don't fall in love so easily," Anne said, but she sounded wary, and frankly she had no idea whether or not this was true.

This cousin of Wilma's was thin and handsome, with hair that was a bit too long, for he cut it himself. He had been taking care of himself for a long time, and was very polite and serious when he greeted them.

"I thought that was you!" he said to Wilma, but his eyes were on Anne. "I don't think we've met before."

"You would remember me," Anne said, and Wilma's cousin laughed.

"I definitely would," he agreed. "I will now."

Anne could see that he was even more handsome than she'd thought when he was far away. She gazed at him through narrowed eyes, judging him, as he told her his story. He was a talker and a storyteller, and that was a quality that caught Anne's attention. His name was Helmut Silberberg and his parents had sent him to Amsterdam from Germany all on his own, after their store had been destroyed on the Night of Broken Glass. He'd taken the train to Amsterdam, where his parents believed he would be safe with his grandparents. He'd left Germany at the age of twelve and had never seen his parents again. If anything, he was the one who took care of his grandfather, who seemed more confused as time went on, and too nervous to venture outside very often.

Wilma's cousin was obsessed with America and was teaching himself English, sometimes refusing to speak Dutch, or even German, his first language. He greeted everyone he knew with a huge *Hello!* It was the word he used more than any other, and his grandfather had given him this nickname, which his friends then took up. He didn't mind it one bit; he disliked his own name, for his given name, Helmut, sounded too Germanic and stodgy. Hello was friendly enough not to be afraid of talking to anyone, and he loved to practice his English, but he seemed shy with Anne, and that made her feel bolder, bold enough to smile at him and to tell him that she wanted to go to America too.

The next morning he was waiting for Anne. After that, she knew he would be there each and every day. That was the way it began. They kept it to themselves, not even telling Wilma. They wanted a secret that felt like hope, at least for a little while. They felt as if they had something no one else had, something that was theirs alone. When Wilma did spy them together, she saw how they stared at each other.

"Is he the one?" Wilma asked dreamily.

"He's the one right now," Anne answered, never being one to tell everything that was in her heart.

✷ ✷ ✷

When no one could see, they held hands, their fingers burning from each other's touch.

"You're on fire," Hello said.

"No, you are," Anne told him, and he didn't disagree. They felt alive when they were together. They felt as if anything could happen. If this had been another time, Anne might have been too young to have a boyfriend, but no one was too young anymore.

"What is it you like about me?" she asked Hello.

"I like that you speak your mind," he told her.

Anne was so alive; she shone with light. She always had a million questions and she never settled for a simple answer. It was clear he couldn't take his eyes off her.

"What are you looking at?" Anne asked, grinning.

"What do you think?" Hello answered. He was interested in what Anne had to say. She didn't hold things back just to be polite, and after spending time with her, all other girls seemed boring to him now.

"I like you even when you argue with me," Hello said.

Anne thought of her parents quarreling and told him that she didn't wish to be like them.

"We'll never be like them," Hello assured her.

Anne leaned in close. "I'm glad you're here," she told him. They held hands, but only for a moment, because perhaps they were too young for this after all.

* * *

When they were alone, Hello told her that he thought that he loved her and Anne didn't know what to say. She wasn't even sure she knew what love was. When she didn't answer, Hello said, "Anne. Did you hear me?"

He was so tall Anne had to look up to see his face. At first she thought he was teasing her. Who talked about love like this, discussing it so openly on a walk to Oase for ice cream, or sitting behind the hedges near the Skyscraper? She was ready to act hurt and insist he was teasing her, but then she saw the expression on his face and realized that he was serious.

"But you don't even know me," Anne told him. "It's only been weeks. You can't love me yet."

Hello grinned when he heard the word *yet*, and in fact Anne was charmed by his declaration and by the way he looked at her. He was the first person to say he loved her, and when she walked beside him her heart beat faster, too fast, she thought sometimes. It seemed that there was something trapped inside her chest when she was with Hello, not one of the black moths she saw in the shadows, but a monarch butterfly. She'd read that they migrated through California, so there were times when the whole world seemed orange and bright.

After Hello's declaration, Anne enjoyed the fact that he was totally infatuated with her, even though she knew it was likely that nothing would come of the flirtation. She'd been interested in other boys before, and she imagined it was likely she would be again, but for now he was the one, and who knew where it might lead, for she found that more and more she cared about his opinion of her. Lately she had taken to biting her nails and she didn't want him to know that she did. She did her best to hide her hands, but Hello took them in his own. There was heat in the palms of their hands every time they touched, and she wondered if this was what her grandmother had meant when she talked about finding someone who was your bashert, a person who was meant for you, two souls who were fated to be together.

"Maybe we could find a way to get to America." Hello had been slowly convincing himself that this was a possibility.

"We would need papers," Anne said. "I've heard my father talking about it. They're not allowing us in."

"Then we could run away. We could camp in the forest and wait for all of this to be over. People do it all the time."

"And some of them die in the forest," Anne told him. She'd overheard someone talking at school. It was difficult to hide in the Netherlands, they'd said, where the land was so flat that as soon as you left the city, it was possible to see for miles. A cousin of one of Anne's classmates had disappeared into the woods attempting to get to Belgium. There was no body to bury, and no one dared to tell his mother. They pretended he was still in the forest and it was there he would always remain.

Hello gave in, at least for now. "Then we'll wait."

Instead of walking her home, Hello accompanied Anne to the alleyway where bicycles were stored. Milk was delivered there in tall metal cans, and there were two cats that were waiting around, one orange and one a tabby cat, even though there were no deliveries anymore.

Anne was good at flirting, funny and at ease with words, and she wasn't easily flustered by boys as many of the girls in her class were. She didn't know why she was so comfortable teasing boys and chatting with them; it was just in her nature to be friendly and sociable. Some of the girls in her class were jealous of her, they said she was conceited, and that she would flirt with just about anyone for the fun of it even if she didn't care a thing about him. The truth was, flirting wasn't much different than acting. But she realized she wasn't flirting this time and she wasn't acting with Hello. She didn't want to care about him too much, because then it would be much too difficult if he decided he was no longer interested.

"I can't love anyone," she said. "I'm just warning you."

Hello stared at her, a hurt expression spreading across his face. Anne bit her tongue and wished she hadn't said that out loud. She wished they had all the time in the world. She wished they were birds that could fly away, but she knew they were not.

"What if you could?" Hello said. He had cheered up thinking that it was only a matter of convincing Anne, and his grin was beautiful; it lit up his face.

"We're too young for love," Anne said.

Hello disagreed and wasn't afraid to say so. "We can't afford to be young. We have to do what we want to do right now."

The next time they met he brought her a white carnation wrapped in brown paper. He'd found it in the rear of a shop in the flower market, tossed into a bin and left to rot. As far as Anne was concerned, she had never seen anything as beautiful as this single flower. The world stopped for a moment. She could never explain why she liked to read so much, how healing it was, how it transformed everything. She forgot everything else all around them now in the alley behind the Skyscraper, the way she forgot everything when she was in the middle of a book. The rest of the world disappeared. The signs forbidding Jews to enter parks, the gardens they weren't allowed to enter. She was someplace else. She was far from here in a place that had no name. The only difference between reading and being with Hello was that this time they were in this together and she wasn't alone. They had been to another place where no one could reach them, but they had been there together.

* * *

"What is true love?" Anne asked her mother. After all, in a matter of weeks she would be thirteen, and everything she knew about romance was a hodgepodge of misinformation told to her at school by the older girls. It was all a mystery, and Anne always liked to know the truth. It made sense to be practical, even about a subject as mystifying as love.

Edith rolled her eyes when asked about the meaning of love and simply continued to fold the laundry.

"Seriously," Anne said when her mother didn't answer. "How would you define it?"

"There's no point in discussing this." She didn't have the heart to talk about love, considering the world around them and the mistakes she herself had made.

"Because I'd like your opinion," Anne said.

Edith hung up a sweater on the line. The soap she was using was harsh, composed of cheap lye, and it turned her hands red. There wasn't much of it left. She had decided not to think about what she would do when it was gone. Perhaps she would use hot water and vinegar, until that was gone too. She couldn't think past that, to having nothing at all.

"If you really want to know, it's something that you find in storybooks," Edith scolded, not meaning to sound as bitter as she did or to show how her fears had overtaken her.

Anne thought about that. "No," she said. "That's not the answer."

"It's my answer," Edith said. "Especially for a girl your age."

Anne said nothing but she knew her mother was wrong. She went to Pim that night and curled up beside him as he read.

"I don't want to interrupt," Anne said to her father. She knew how annoying it was when someone tried to speak to her when she was reading.

"You would never be interrupting." Pim put down his book. He had given his daughters very little time lately, he had been so busy with the secret plan of what they would do next. He and Edith discussed it late at night, in whispers, and in some ways their secret had made them closer. It was a last chance for all of them, and they felt it inside them, and sometimes they held hands in bed and stayed up together to see the morning light.

"What's love?" Anne asked.

Pim didn't have to think twice. He immediately answered, "It's what I feel for you and for Margot."

Anne laughed. "Thank you. But what does it mean?"

"What does it mean? Darling, it means I would do anything for you. That's what love is."

"What about romantic love?" It was hard for Anne to discuss this with her father because she knew he still thought of her as his little girl. She explained that she was talking about people who felt love for each other not because they had to, because they were family, but because they had fallen in love without ever expecting to, without having to.

"Ah, that." Pim sighed. "That is different for everyone, Anne."

They exchanged a look.

"I mean for me," Anne said.

"Some people have it and some people don't," Pim answered. "You'll have it, Anne." He seemed convinced of this.

Anne laughed again and shook her head. "How can you know that?"

"Because I know who you are. Because you're special."

Anne used to believe everything he said, and she still wanted to, but for some reason she couldn't. She didn't care if she was special anymore. She just wanted time to grow up. Outside their house everything was changing. Those few birds that hadn't flown away were falling from the sky and she'd never seen the magpie again. Fish went on sleeping; they sank to the bottom of the canals as the weather grew warm and Anne couldn't help but wonder if fish could drown. There was no one to ask. No one knew anything. Not about love or fish or about the future. Not even Pim knew. Not anymore. All that Anne knew was that every morning Hello was waiting for her at the bicycle shed, and they walked and talked as if the rest of the world didn't exist. Perhaps that was what it meant to be in love. For a little while at least it was possible to forget everyone else.

CHAPTER TWELVE

At last, it was the best day of the year, Anne's birthday, June 12. She woke at six, but she made herself stay in bed until daylight flickered through the window. She wanted to savor her first day of being thirteen. It would never happen again. This was the birthday that meant she was no longer a child, not that she had felt like one for some time, but this day made it official. Thirteen was a mystical and magical number. *Love* and *unity* were said to equal thirteen, a lucky number. But the truth was, nothing was lucky anymore. Starting the next month, at least one hundred seven thousand Jews began to be deported from the Netherlands to death camps such as Auschwitz so that more than 75 percent of all Jews in the country would be murdered by the end of the war. Out on the street, you could only talk in whispers if you dared to speak at all. More and more babies would be left with Christian families who would take them in and raise them as their own, at least until the war had ended.

Still, on this day Anne could have hope in the future, she could try her best to imagine her future now that she was no longer a child. She ran into the dining room, where her cat, Moortje, was waiting for her.

"You're awake too early!" Pim cried, although he himself had risen before the sun to prepare for this day. The first present Anne saw was the diary she'd wished for from Blankevoort, the bookstore nearby, and she was utterly delighted to know that Pim had remembered how much she'd wanted it.

"You knew just the right present!" Anne cried as she opened the diary to the first blank page. It was perfect. Maybe she could be a writer after all.

Her parents had done their best to give her all that they could this year, and there were other presents as well. A blue blouse, some grape juice, which was difficult to find nowadays, a puzzle, some face cream, a bit of money, a plate of biscuits she herself had baked the day before as a gift to herself and her school friends, and a strawberry tart her mother had baked, for it was strawberry season. All the gifts were so special. That night, Anne wrote in the diary. She closed the door and sat in bed and for the first time she felt as if she wasn't completely alone.

After walking to school with Hanneli, each of them taking thirteen steps and then stopping and starting again as a way to celebrate Anne's new age, Anne handed out the rest of the biscuits at school. In return, the other students danced around Anne as if she were a birthday queen, and the truth of it was, she enjoyed the attention. Her friends came to the apartment after school and gave her a gorgeous book, *Dutch Sagas and Legends*. It was Volume II, so she planned to exchange some other books for Volume I.

It was difficult to celebrate a birthday properly these days, but Pim insisted, and on Sunday they had a small party. Hanneli and Jacque were there. Anne didn't like to be alone so she was glad for the crowd; she often had the odd sense that she would vanish if no one was there with her, but now she found she felt alone even when she was with her friends.

Some of her friends found her more and more overwhelming. They said that she took charge and often made you do things her way, that she was more stubborn and opinionated all the time, and perhaps she was. Anne served her friends plates of cake. She knew her parents wanted the best for her, even now that it was difficult to celebrate anything. She looked out the window and saw the black moths in the trees where the birds used to be. She wished that she and Hello lived in another time, and that they could go to the sea and find a boat and disappear to someplace brand new, somewhere where they could do as they pleased. She longed for a future they could make for themselves, one in which the bombs had never fallen. She wished they could be anywhere else but here.

Sitting there, among her friends, Anne had the feeling that no one knew her, and that she'd never truly had a friend in her life. They were all enjoying themselves, and she couldn't eat a bite of her own birthday cake. She thought of the magpies that never migrated to another country and were now hiding in chimneys, and of the baby rabbits she had recently found beneath the hedges in the square waiting for their mother, who was in the center of the road, hit by a car. Anne had thought all the rabbits were gone, but these had managed to return. She had sat beside them, crying, not knowing what to do. Her mother had come out and called for her.

"Do you know what time it is?" Edith had cried.

"There are baby rabbits," Anne had called back.

"Anne." Edith had sounded a bit panicked. "It's eight o'clock. Come this minute!"

Anne had gone inside, and the next day, when she went to search for them, they were gone. Things disappeared, she knew that now, she knew it every time she walked through the dining room, where her grandmother had slept. People in their neighborhood would soon begin to vanish, the ones who were in the Resistance, the ones who had wealth the Germans wanted, the ones who had done nothing at all, the ones who had been in the wrong place at the wrong time because life wasn't fair, and when dealing with people like the Nazis, nothing made sense.

If anything, turning thirteen had made Anne feel more alone. She had thought it would change everything for the better, but it hadn't. She felt as if she was now supposed to know what she should do with her life, but given the way the world was, she couldn't see the possibilities of what her future might be. She did her best to be grateful, for her parents had succeeded in giving her a lovely birthday party. Anne was stunned when she was given other wonderful gifts. Two brooches, a bookmark, sweets, and two books she wanted, including *Daisy's Mountain Holiday*, and the book from the bookstall that was so beautifully illustrated, *The Myths of Greece and Rome*.

"It's a good thing I bought this book when I did," Pim told Anne, patting her hair as if she were still his little girl. Anne understood his meaning. They had walked past the Oudemanhuispoort Book Market to see that all the Jewish booksellers were gone, and the books they'd sold had either been hidden or destroyed, and Anne remembered what Clara DePina had said about words. They could be remembered even when everything else was gone. No Jewish writers could be read; it was a crime to do so, and yet, despite this, Anne kept the fact that she wanted to be a writer to herself. It seemed preposterous. She was only a young girl with nothing to say, and yet the best of her gifts was the diary. She could already tell it would be a trusted friend she could tell her secrets to.

Because Jews were not allowed in theaters, Pim had brought home a movie projector and a copy of the Rin Tin Tin movie. It was the story about a faithful dog and a world where good people were easily saved, and they all watched in the dining room, rapt as the images flickered on the wall. No one knew Anne cried halfway through the film because she wished they could step inside it and be half a world away.

* * *

Anne might have been thirteen and nearly a grown woman, but lately her math teacher treated her as if she was a misbehaving child, giving her extra work in return for her not paying attention in class. When Anne continued to talk during lessons, unable to sit still or be quiet, and had been warned countless times to stop talking, her teacher required that she write an essay titled "A Chatterbox." How unlike her sister she was, for Margot's work was always brilliant, with excellent grades, and she never had to be reprimanded, whereas Anne kept talking. A day later, she was asked to write a second essay, which he titled "An Incorrigible Chatterbox."

When she still had not stopped talking to her friends, she was assigned to write a third, called "Quack, Quack, Quack, Said Mistress Chatterback."

"Would you rather me say nothing at all?" Anne asked.

"At times, yes. For instance, when I'm speaking."

The class all laughed at that remark.

Their teacher had a good sense of humor, so Anne, with the help of her friend Sanne, who was so good at rhyming, wrote something that she thought might amuse the other students and their teacher as well. Maybe she could be a writer; maybe she could start right now.

"'Quack, quack, quack,' said Mistress Chatterback," the teacher read aloud to the class. Even he thought the poem Anne had written about being unable to keep silent was well done and funny, and after that her teacher no longer seemed annoyed when Anne talked to her friends.

"Just keep it down," he said. That was the power of writing, Anne realized, it could make people understand you, it could bring them over to your side, it could show them you were more than a silly girl who couldn't stop talking.

Anne sometimes wrote in class, her arm stretched out

on her desk, hiding the paper. The girls around her noticed what she was doing and were curious. "Can we read it?" several of them asked, but Anne shook her head, annoyed at being interrupted. She was too busy to answer. She was in her grandmother's garden watching the bees. She was sitting with Oma in the dining room. She was with the boy who was waiting for her every morning, someone who might love her someday.

"Just a line or two?" the other girls asked. "Just a look?"

"It's none of your business," Anne said in a voice that made it clear she wouldn't change her mind.

People said she was cross and ill-humored and had to have things her way or not at all. She hadn't changed one bit, they said, but that wasn't the truth. They didn't know she cried at night as she looked out the window watching for rabbits and not seeing a single one. At home, she was often so quiet that her parents worried that she wasn't her usual talkative self. Ever since her grandmother had been gone, Anne felt sure that her heart would be much easier to break than it had been before. She still spied the black moth every now and then, just outside the window. The moth was likely nothing;

it wasn't sorrow or death or grief, it couldn't tell her future or change her past, and when she looked again there was nothing but the shadow of the leaves. Despite her sadness, she arose each morning ready to face the day. She would speak up in class. She would read every book she could. She would meet Hello after school. She knew what her Oma's answer would be if she asked what she should do now that she was thirteen and no longer a child.

Enjoy every day, live it as if it were your last, don't think too much about the future or the past, run to meet the boy who is waiting for you in the square, read every book you can, write every night, look at the moonlight, do all that you can to stay alive.

CHAPTER THIRTEEN

People had been crying in the street that day. A neighbor's husband had been beaten without mercy and taken away, for what alleged wrongdoing, no one knew. *You cannot reason with people who are unreasonable,* Oma had once told Anne. *You cannot expect the Nazis to act like normal people. Evil people tell themselves a story they come to believe. They tell themselves they are good, and everyone else is inhuman. They tell themselves they are doing what heaven would will them to do.*

The anguished family of the man who'd been beaten was told to get down on their knees on the sidewalk and be silent during his arrest.

"What did he do?" the man's wife had cried, but no one had had an answer. A policeman hit her with his gun and she looked up at him, dazed. Anne had opened the door and she'd stood on the stairs. Everything changed; nothing was safe. She saw the man's wife crying in the grass where there used to be rabbits. She saw blood on the sidewalk and in between the blades of grass. She saw a hundred black moths underneath the bushes, just waiting for the night.

"Come inside," Anne's mother had called from the doorway, and for once Anne did as she was told. She ran inside, terrified. She ran away just as she had on the night she'd found the rabbits. They hadn't talked about it afterward, but Edith had kept her eye on Anne. The world was a brutal place and the wife of their neighbor had to be taken away by her family, for she had refused to move, or perhaps she couldn't, perhaps she'd given up.

"I wish you hadn't seen that," Edith said. She wore her hair pulled back and her face was pale. Lately, she had on the same dress day after day, washing it in the sink and hanging it in the kitchen to dry overnight.

"I'm fine," Anne told her mother.

"Are you?"

In fact, Anne was shivering as if it were winter. She looked out the window. The square was empty, but there was a shadow in the place where the neighbor had knelt down to beg for mercy.

"We should have done something," Anne said.

"We are doing something." Anne looked at her mother, confused, but her mother looked sure of herself. "We're refusing to believe the story they're telling about us."

School had let out and the air was hot and the sky was a vivid blue. There didn't seem to be any birds in the trees; even the magpies in their nests were quiet, but what was wrong with quiet? It was better than sirens, far better than strangers knocking at your door. They would go day by day. Maybe time would move faster and they would be in a future where there was more kindness than cruelty, where evil was defeated and birds sang in the trees, and a girl could stay out past eight o'clock in the evening without fear that she would be arrested.

On Saturday, Anne went to the Oase ice cream parlor with her friends. They had such a good time it was as if the world outside didn't matter, at least for a while. Hello walked her home after taking her to meet his grandfather, who seemed fine but old-fashioned, and on Sunday morning he came over to visit. The day was hot and they sat outside on the roof. No one else was in the house and they held hands and ignored their books and laughed to think no one would find them, at least not for a few hours. They didn't even have time to be young and they knew it.

Anne still saw Hello almost every day, and at last he convinced her that he should meet her parents, who found him to be so intelligent and polite they didn't say no when he asked if he and Anne could go out for a walk after they'd had tea and biscuits in what was now the dining room again. Edith pulled Anne aside and said, "So is this the one you're going to marry?"

They both laughed, but then Anne looked over at Hello and felt her heart beating against her chest.

"He would be a good choice," Edith said.

Anne's mother was acting as if there was very little time left, as if major decisions had to be made right away, or else they might never be made at all. Anne wanted to tell her the truth, but she couldn't bring herself to speak her fears aloud. *Everything is brand new, how could I know what love is yet? Shouldn't I have my whole life ahead of me? Shouldn't I fall in love a dozen times over and have my heart broken and break someone else's heart in return? Shouldn't I have all the time in the world?*

Anne and Hello left the apartment as soon as it was polite to do so. They ran around the corner to Blankevoort Bookstore, where they gazed through the window and pointed out the books they'd like to read. Then they walked around the neighborhood telling each other jokes. After a while, Hello took Anne's hand and it wasn't so funny anymore. She could feel the heat of his blood and her own blood as well. She could feel herself grow tongue-tied when she usually couldn't stop talking. Hello's cousin Wilma had taken Anne aside a few days earlier to tell her how much Hello liked her, and Anne could tell it was even more than that. He now told Anne his previous girlfriend wasn't interesting the way Anne was. The other girl was sweet and lovely, but she wasn't full of life the way Anne was. He'd explained that his grandfather said Anne was too young for Hello, but how could the old man know the first thing about her?

Hello's grandfather wanted everything to stay the same, he wanted the old ways and the old rules, but those things had disappeared. Right and wrong were not clear anymore. The Dutch police could no longer be trusted, for they worked hand in hand with the Nazis, arresting enemies of the Germans, those who had not committed any crime other than being themselves. Nothing was the same and there were other choices to be made now, matters of life and death. Hello told Anne he was meeting with Zionists who believed that their only chance for survival would be in returning to their homeland. His grandfather was angry about that too. Jerusalem was far away and too foreign, and he believed there were radicals there who would only get a boy like Hello in trouble. Hello had stopped telling his grandfather his thoughts after their last argument, and now he felt that Anne was the only one he could really talk to. He took her hand and didn't let go and something happened to the time. It was as if for that one evening they really did have all the time in the world. Before they knew it, it was after eight o'clock and the streets were empty.

They ran through the gathering dark, through shadows on the side streets. No bicycles, no cars, no one else out. Thankfully, they didn't come upon any soldiers or police. The world seemed deserted, and Anne's blood felt even hotter than before. Her face was flushed and her dark hair had become tangled in the humid air. Hello was still holding her hand and he ran so fast Anne felt she might rise up into the air, but she kept up with him.

They were out of breath when they reached number 37 Merwedeplein, stopping on the edge of the square that faced the Franks' apartment building.

"Okay?" Hello said.

Anne nodded. She could see someone behind the curtains. They were waiting for her.

"I'll come by tomorrow," Hello promised as Anne went in through the door.

Pim was there in the hallway, furious. He was so rarely angry at her that tears streamed down Anne's face as her father told her how wrong it was of her to stay out so late. It wasn't a game the Germans were playing. It occurred to Anne that she had been acting like a child, and she was mortified.

"I'm so sorry," she told her father.

"Sorry is not enough anymore," Pim admonished her. He didn't tell her that he had heard that on Friday, the 26th of June, the Jewish Council had been told that all Jews between the ages of sixteen and forty would be sent to work camps in Germany. It began with little more than three hundred taken for the camps each day, but that was only the beginning. More and more people were called up every day.

You could not be found wandering on the street in a world where such things happened. Pim made her give him her solemn promise that she would always be back before dark and that she would never be late again. *Be late and you might never be found again, not if we searched the whole world over. Don't let us lose you this way.*

✳ ✳ ✳

Hello came back the next Sunday to their meeting place in the square. It was July 5, and as they sprawled out in the grass,

Anne told him the myths that her father had studied when he was at university, stories of boys who flew too close to the sun and girls who lived underground beneath a twisted tangle of trees. They counted the clouds in the sky. One for the past, one for the present, one for the future. If they ever made it to California, they would go directly to the Pacific Ocean; they both agreed on that. Anne didn't say she thought this destination was only a dream. "You'll have to change your name," she said as if it might really happen. They went through a list of American-sounding names. Kirk. Eric. Stephen. But for now he was Hello, the boy who understood what it was like to want to run away. His grandfather had him sleep in the closet, in case the Germans came for him in the middle of the night. It was ridiculous, and they laughed because Hello was much too tall to fit in the closet. All the same, he did as his grandfather demanded, even though he often hit his head on the ceiling.

Hello didn't leave Anne until he had to go have lunch with his grandfather; he loved the contrary old man who was no longer able to see to his own meals, but he promised to return to visit Anne in the afternoon. Anne watched

Hello lope across the square; he always seemed to be going somewhere fast. She didn't head for home until he had disappeared. She understood his grandfather's fears and why he forced his beloved grandson to sleep in the closet. Someone might take him and arrest him in the middle of the night, or he would run off and disappear. Hello was such a good storyteller, not unlike her father, and he'd told her of traveling to the Netherlands by himself when he was only twelve and having to run away from Nazi guards. When they were together, he looked at Anne as if he knew she was the one, even though it was much too soon to make a serious choice. They had time to make a decision as important as that. Love took time and choosing the right person did too.

Anne wondered if her mother had once had a list of wishes for the future just as Anne had and if she'd written down the very same one that Anne herself wanted most of all.

Love someone.

"Why do you always ask me who I will marry?" Anne asked her mother as she helped with the laundry. They were hanging the sheets on a rope strung up on the rooftop, but they would bring them in before they had completely dried.

White sheets on the roof might bring attention to them and make people wonder, if they had clean bedding, what else did they have? Silver candlesticks, gold earrings, coins hidden under the sofa?

"Why shouldn't I ask?" Edith wanted to know.

Anne shrugged. "Maybe I won't get married at all."

"You will," Edith told her.

"How do you know that I will?" Her mother couldn't know how she felt about Hello or how she felt about the future. She wanted so much she didn't think it was possible to get it all.

"I know because you have love inside of you," Edith assured Anne. She almost said *Because you're special. That's how I know.*

The sheets they'd hung to dry were white and they looked like clouds against the blue sky, and Anne didn't say anything, but it was true. Whatever else she wanted, she knew that she wanted to love someone who would love her back, someone who would know her for who she was.

Anne went up to the rooftop to read. She needed time alone, time to slip into the other world she found in novels and now in her diary. Her father was visiting the widow of an acquaintance who had just passed away at the Jewish Hospital and Margot was down in their bedroom. Anne wanted to be alone with her thoughts, and that was probably why she didn't hear the bell when it rang. The day was clear and hot, but Anne saw something black in the sky, and for a moment she thought it was the magpie returning; she thought it was a good sign. But it was a storm that would arrive by morning, with so much rain falling that the streets would flood. If it was a sign of anything, it was a mark that this was the day when their lives would change. It would happen now on an ordinary afternoon when sunlight flooded the rooftop. The doorbell rang and an unfamiliar man's voice was drifting up. It was a summer afternoon and everything was the same, and then, before they knew what was happening, nothing would ever be the same again.

Both sisters heard their mother cry out after she closed the door, hurrying with the latch. But it was one lock, not a thousand, and it would never keep out what was waiting for them. A man had just left their house. He walked in a strange way, the way a goblin might, but he was a policeman, an everyday policeman who was posted in this neighborhood, sent to deliver messages from the government.

Margot had run out of her room and now she and their mother were huddled together. She sensed that something terrible had happened; she could feel it in her bones. Edith grew pale and blurted, "It's a call-up for the labor camp."

Margot had heard rumors about what it meant to be called up by a government order. They had all heard the rumors. They would be told they would return, but most vanished and never did.

✶ ✶ ✶

"Go to your room and don't answer the door," Edith told Margot. "Not for anyone." She told her that she was going to see Hermann van Pels, Pim's partner, a man whose advice she trusted and with whom Otto and Edith had discussed a plan of going into hiding.

The sisters met inside their bedroom without a word. The world seemed upside down. Margot was still holding the notice in her hands and her hands were shaking. "Father has received a call-up notice from the SS."

"Maybe he won't have to go," Anne said. She realized that Margot was crying, and she did her best to comfort her sister. It was always so odd to see Margot cry—it wasn't like her to fall apart so easily. "They won't catch Pim. He'll run away," Anne assured her sister. "He'll go to England."

"It's too late to go to England. They're not letting Jews in." Margot had stopped crying by then and she wiped her tearstained face. Her voice was softer than usual, so soft that Anne could barely hear her. "Anyway, the notice wasn't for him."

Anne looked at her sister, in a daze. For some reason she could hardly breathe.

"It was for me," Margot said. She looked paler than ever; she looked like a shadow in a dream. "I'm the one who's been called up for a labor camp."

Anne shook her head. She was sure of herself. She had to be. "No. It can't be for you." Her beautiful, kind sister could not have been called up to a labor camp, a place where the conditions were unbearable, unlivable, with very few survivors. It was impossible. It simply couldn't be. Not in a world where good was supposed to win out over evil. "You misread it. You must have."

Margot shook her head. "It's my name. Mama didn't want you to know. She thought it would frighten you and she wanted to protect you. Even if it's only for a little while longer."

"Why did she tell you then?" Without realizing it, Anne had begun to shiver. It might as well not be summer anymore.

"Because it's *my* life. She had no choice. She had to tell me."

Margot was to report to the SS Central Office for Jewish Emigration, where the Nazis organized the deportations. Here, deportees would collect their train tickets and a list of items to bring along. Sheets and a blanket and food for several days, along with a cup, a spoon, two changes of clothes. Their suitcase must have their name and date of birth written on it, along with the word *Holland*.

"They're taking anyone sixteen and older," Margot said, her voice ragged. She didn't seem like the sister Anne knew, calm and beautiful and well-mannered. "Soon they'll take everyone."

"No. The Americans will get here," Anne insisted.

"When? Do you see them?" Margot said. "Have they arrived?"

Anne had no time to answer. Before she could, there was a knock at the door. Someone was on their front steps. The girls moved closer together, startled. They slipped to the floor and kept their heads down. There were shadows all over the walls. Moths were in the corners. Echoes rang outside.

"Is it them?" Anne whispered, fearing the government officials. "Are they back?"

The knocking went on, and then Anne's name was called. She was crouched down, shivering, her hands over her ears. It took a moment for her to recognize Hello's voice. Anne had forgotten he had promised to come back in the afternoon after he gave his grandfather his lunch. Anne went to stand so she could let him in, but Margot pulled her back down to crouch on the floor. "Don't open the door to anyone," Margot reminded her.

"He's come to see me!" Anne said to her sister, ready to leap up and go to the door.

Margot shook her head. "It doesn't matter. You can't speak to him."

"What will he think?" Anne felt a rising panic inside her. She already knew the answer. He would think she didn't care and that he meant nothing to her. She knew he was in love with her, and she didn't want to break his heart or her own. She hadn't taken him seriously, at least not yet. If they'd met some other time they would have had all the time in the world. Now it was different. There was no time at all.

"He can't know what we're doing," Margot whispered. "Later he'll understand."

He would never understand, but what could Anne do?

"I'll lose him," she said so softly she didn't think her sister would hear, but Margot reached for her and they held hands as they listened to Hello continue to call out, sounding more and more upset.

"Anne? Are you home? Is everything all right?" He knocked on the door, then he slammed his palm against the wood. "Anne!" he called.

Anne drew her knees up and kept her head down, her hands over her ears. Would he really know how much she wanted to run and open the door? Would he ever understand? In a while, the noise stopped. He had gone away. She had no idea what would happen next, but she felt as if she'd never hear his voice again.

Edith came home with Hermann van Pels, and they sat in the kitchen waiting for Otto to return. They talked in whispers about their secret plan to go into hiding before anyone was called up. Otto and Mr. Van Pels had been preparing a hiding place and Pim had been planning for the family to go there in ten days, but now the call-up had happened, before they had managed to vanish. When Otto arrived home, he told them they couldn't wait any longer. Mr. Van Pels and his wife, Auguste, and their son, Peter, who had turned fifteen, would join them soon.

The girls didn't know where the secret place was, perhaps it was a swan's nest out by the river near the hotel in the countryside, or maybe they would flee to an abandoned house by the seaside where the North Sea would roar at night, or to a farm where there would be fresh milk and cheese and they could sneak out at night to search for cabbages and potatoes. But Pim still refused to tell them where they'd be going. It was better for them not to know where their destination was; then they couldn't let it slip to anyone by mistake. When they left in the morning, they would leave a note for anyone who might look for them, suggesting they had plans to travel to family in Switzerland. Their friends would have no reason to doubt them, and the police would have no reason to search for them. They would vanish until the world was safe once more. You never knew who might be watching, so they kept the curtains closed, day and night, and Otto told no one of his intentions, other than those who were directly involved in his plans.

It can't be happening, Anne thought, but it was. This could not be their last night at home, but it was. Anne packed her new diary and then added a hodgepodge of belongings. She could hardly think of what she might need in this unknown place they were headed for, and so she'd taken the first things she saw. Handkerchiefs, schoolbooks, a comb, and some letters. At the last minute, she took the blue ribbon she had found at the river when she and Pim were in the countryside, and she stuffed it into her coat pocket. Everything seemed like a memory to her now.

Miep and Jan and Otto's partner Kleiman came at eleven, after curfew. They had agreed to help them, buying their groceries and keeping their whereabouts secret for as long as necessary. Now, at this late hour, they picked up the last bags of belongings to take to the hiding place. The fact that there were such good people in the world left the family in tears, for if discovered, anyone helping them would be arrested. Bringing them groceries, helping move their belongings, all of it could come with a death sentence if they were caught.

"Are you sure?" Anne heard her mother ask Miep as she was about to leave.

"Of course. I could not be any more sure. You are my family now."

This was the way it was; there were good people and there were evil people; even though you couldn't tell them apart by sight, you could tell the difference with your heart. You could feel who loved you and who was willing to risk everything to save you.

✷ ✷ ✷

Their mother woke them at five thirty in the morning, when it was still black as night. It was raining so hard they could barely see outside.

"Wear everything you can," Edith told Anne. "It may be all you have for a long time."

They talked in whispers and the sisters did as they were told. Anne did not talk back, she wasn't a chatterbox, she was a girl who did as she was told. It was the day they would disappear into the place where the birds went to hide in the treetops. That's where the magpies were, high in the tallest trees, so far away they couldn't be seen.

Anne pulled on two vests, along with three pairs of pants, a dress, a skirt, a jacket, a raincoat, a cap, a wool scarf, two pairs of stockings, and heavy shoes. They could not go all together; an entire family walking through the city might draw suspicion, it might be obvious that they were together in order to flee from the Germans. No one said another word. Silence was everything, it was unbreakable, it was all they had to protect themselves. Margot left first with Miep; they went on bicycles, riding off into the unknown. Fog was covering the city and everything was gray as rain fell. Margot had removed the yellow star from her coat, hoping that no one would stop her, knowing how brave Miep was merely to accompany her on this dark morning.

Anne waved to them, then stood with her back against the door, still not having any idea where their secret hiding place was. When they disappeared down the street, Anne felt as if she had lost them forever. Had they disappeared into the underworld? Would they be caught by soldiers on their way into hiding? She thought of smoke and ashes, and how something could go up in flames and disappear in an instant.

Anne's mother came up beside her. "You'll see them in a few hours," Edith said.

"Why do I feel like I won't?" Anne bit her lip. She refused to cry. She might not ever cry again if she could will herself not to.

"You will," Edith assured her. "I promise you on my life."

They had been so little when they'd first moved into 37 Merwedeplein, but they were young women now. Thirteen and sixteen. Lucky numbers that seemed very unlucky on this day. Standing in her room for the last time, Anne wished they had left long ago. They should have flown away before the bombs fell, while they still had the chance to escape, but they hadn't predicted what was to come. The future was a mystery until you were standing right inside it. You could only see it clearly when you looked backward. Now they saw everything that had led to this day. The signs, the stars, the rules, the vanishing of every part of their lives except their love for one another.

There had been broiling-hot weather all week, but the cool rain that was falling had broken the heat wave and Anne felt chilled as she took her small satchel, for her mother had told her a large suitcase might draw attention.

"Hurry up," her mother called. "There's no time left."

As they readied themselves to go, Anne's father told her not to talk once they left home; they would walk quickly and act as if they were doing nothing out of the ordinary. They would carry bags and satchels, as if they'd been to a market. Halfway out the door, Anne stopped, panicked. Her cat, Moortje, was still upstairs.

"We can't leave her!" Anne had the urge to run upstairs, to go out onto the roof and stay there with her cat.

"The neighbors will take care of her," her father assured her.

If Anne had spoken, she might have broken down. Her beloved little cat would be here waiting for her.

"You know it's true," Pim said to comfort Anne. "And Moortje will be happier here, in the neighborhood she knows. And we'll come back."

Anne looked at her father. She wanted to believe him.

"We'll come back," he insisted, but Anne could tell from the tone of his voice. He might have believed all would be well once upon a time, but now he wasn't sure. Anything could happen. The whole world could disappear, and where would one cat be then? Where would their family be, falling through the darkness into the underworld, holding on to one another as best they could?

And then they left, just as her mother had promised they would. It was seven thirty in the morning on the 6th of July. They left the breakfast dishes on the table, so that it would seem they had left in a hurry, without any plans.

＊　＊　＊

Anne was not allowed to say goodbye to anyone; it was too dangerous. She merely vanished. The next day, her friends

Hanneli and Jacque would arrive to find her gone. They phoned and hoped she would send them a letter or a secret note, but there was nothing. Hello never went back, and Anne wouldn't have expected him to. After he stopped knocking at the door, he'd stood there with the sun in his eyes and he'd stared up at her window with a look of inexpressible longing. It was over, and he knew it, and it brought him little comfort to know they were too young anyway. In another world they might have fallen in love, but this was not that world. Anne hoped he would disappear from the city before he was called up to a labor camp. She hoped he would go somewhere where the sea was blue. She hoped he would think of her when he was far from here.

When they were ready to go, Anne and her parents walked out into the pale rain, not daring to speak as they made their way through the neighborhood. All three were drenched by the time they came to the canal. They had crossed the city to the old section. The hiding place wasn't far away, it wasn't by the seaside or on a farm. It was in her father's brick office building at 263 Prinsengracht. There were two empty floors that had mostly been unused. This was the place that Otto had been secretly readying in case of an emergency and a day he'd hoped would never come. Now it was here, the day of vanishing, the day when they had to save themselves. They would hear the chiming of the nearby Westertoren clock that rang from Amsterdam's tallest church steeple every quarter of an hour. Anne already knew she would find comfort in the sound.

"No matter what, I won't leave you," Edith told her daughter as they approached the building.

"I know you won't," Anne said. It was so strange that you could be so angry at your mother for so long, and then, all at once, let it go so that every breath you took felt different.

They were holding hands, something they rarely did. Edith held on so tightly that Anne knew that if she ever disappeared her mother would search the whole world over until she found her. Even if they traveled through forests filled with thorns, through fields of ice, through the underworld. They would go there together.

"We'll be fine," Edith said. "We'll be hidden."

Anne nodded, but she didn't answer. All she knew was this: Her life would never be the same. She saw a trail of leaves on the brick sidewalk, fallen from the sky in the rainstorm, leading them to the brick building. The day when everything changed for her wasn't the day when the bombs fell, or the day when the queen disappeared, or the day when the books were taken off the shelves. It wasn't the day when Jews were no longer allowed to sit on park benches or enter public buildings or the day when they had to wear yellow stars on their coats. In her life, today was the day that was unlike any other, when one world ended and another began, when she held her mother's hand, when her father was crying, when she didn't care if she would be beautiful or not, when she just wanted to grow up, that's all she would ask for now. It was the day when the present became the past, and the future was too dark to see, when the rain finally stopped and the magpie sat in the tree, following her for the last time.

The streets were empty at this hour. People were in their houses, many still in their beds, fast asleep. Anne thought of Persephone trapped in the underworld, hidden from everything she had ever known, waiting for spring. She was thankful she'd brought her diary. She peered into her bag to make sure it hadn't been dropped as they'd hurried along to their hiding place. She had a sudden, strange stir of fear worrying that she had lost it, but it was there, and she was overjoyed. Just seeing it gave her hope. She would write it all down.

Even though the rain had let up, the air was still damp and smelled like trees. The leaves were so heavy they fell to the ground like clouds, as if it were already autumn. It was then Anne realized they weren't leaves at all but the black moths that fluttered downward, their wings too drenched to fly. She felt a pain in her chest, and each breath was difficult. She wanted the life she'd had. She wanted the world to stay the same. She wanted good to win over evil and monsters to be trapped and kept locked up in chains. Anne wondered if she would ever feel the rain on her face again, if she would ever again stand beneath an elm tree. In this area there were already many families in hiding, teenagers and young men and mothers and children whose names Anne would never know. She didn't know what it felt like when they'd stood out on the street for the last time, but perhaps it wasn't so different than it was for her.

She remembered everything. There was more than bombs

and beatings and rules. There was the life she had lived. There was the cloudy sky and the rabbits in the grass, there was the memory of a boy who knocked at the door of their apartment when she couldn't answer, there was the river they'd skated on and the elm tree where there was once a magpie who had flown away and hadn't returned until this day. She remembered the bricks on the sidewalk, the dark water of the canal, the look on her mother's face, the puddles of rain. The last moment of anything is one you never forget.

Miep was standing at the door, waiting for them. Quick as she could, Anne took a piece of paper and a pencil from her pocket. She wrote out her wish, reached for the blue ribbon, then ran to an elm tree nearby and tied the slip of paper to the lowest branch. Her mother was watching her. She didn't hurry Anne as she usually did, even though the hour for hiding had come. The paper tied to the tree moved back and forth like a bell with no sound.

"It's just a wish," Anne said.

"Good." Her mother nodded. There was some dust or grass in her eyes. Anne knew what that was like. You had to hide your tears when it happened. "I hope it comes true."

Remember us. That is what she wished for. That is what she'd written down. *Remember me.*

* * *

When Anne went inside, she didn't dare to glance back. She would only look forward now. Out on the street there was the world where they had lived. How beautiful it had been. They'd had everything before and she would remember every bit of it even though she couldn't go back there now. The warehouse smelled liked cinnamon and cloves and pepper. It was so dark inside it was as if they had fallen into the world below. They would be going up a steep set of stairs to the rooms where they would stay until the war was over; Margot was already there. They might see the trees from their window if they moved the shade; it made the whole world look green, as if there was a forest just outside the door now that they were in a world of their own. It was happening all over the city, secret worlds of hidden people who had no other way to escape. For now, there was a place to be, a place that was in the middle of the city and yet was so far away from the rest of life it might have been another country.

The day was just beginning and there was a great deal of work to do. They would hang curtains and make up the bare mattresses with clean sheets and then Anne would begin to decorate the walls of her small bedroom with her postcard collection that Pim had brought from home as a surprise. But before all that, before she looked at the room where she would sleep for the next two years, before she wondered if anything was ever fair, before she lost everyone she had ever loved or mourned for, before she thought of the stars in the sky she would never see, before she wept over the future that was waiting for them, before she took out her diary, she turned and closed the door.

What We Will Remember

Blue ice, bookstores, your grandmother sleeping in the dining room, the ice cream parlor, your classroom, the books you read, the hotel by the river, the photographs of movie stars taped over your bed, the magpie in the tree, your sister at the door signaling for you to hurry, finally understanding that your mother would search the whole world over for you if you ever vanished, the future you dreamed of, your hope that deep inside people were good.

You knew you had to write it all down. Once you did, your world wouldn't disappear, your grandmother would still be calling your name, your father would be assuring you that you were beautiful, there would still be a boy waiting for you on a street corner who might have been your first love if there had been enough time.

There you still are sitting on your bed, writing, knowing a secret you can tell the world.

Love is everything, love is everywhere, it's the one thing they can never take away from you.

* * *

Anne perished at the age of fifteen in Bergen-Belsen concentration camp soon after her sister, Margot, died, approximately two months before British forces liberated the camp.

Holocaust, from the Greek, holokauston, an offering consumed by fire.

Afterword

In the year when I was twelve, I discovered many of the books that have meant the most to me, books that changed my life. This is true for many of us. At twelve, we are becoming the adult readers we will one day be, and hopefully, it is a time when we have the freedom to walk into a library or a bookstore and choose any book we wish to read. We can experiment with books, find the voices that speak to us, and see life all around us as something brand new.

The book that affected me more than any other was *The Diary of a Young Girl*, by Anne Frank. It changed the way I looked at the world. It changed the person I was and the person I would become. I read the diary in 1964. It was only twenty years after Anne Frank was murdered by the Nazis at Bergen-Belsen concentration camp, and yet I had heard very little about the Holocaust and the systematic genocide of the Jews in Europe. Looking back, I believe people in my family, New York Jews who had emigrated from Russia, wanted to look ahead to the future rather than remember the tragedies of the past, like many other people who had come of age during World War II. My father never spoke about fighting at the front in France, or the traumas he experienced there. The generation that had seen the atrocities of World War II wanted to protect their children from the reality of the brutality of the war.

These were the days when people who had cancer often preferred not to say the word aloud, instead calling the disease "the big C," as if speaking the word *cancer* aloud might bring bad luck. Family secrets were kept secret, and children were protected from hard truths. Keep quiet about your problems and keep your grief to yourself, that was what we were told. It was a new world, and many people wanted to see only the bright future they were hoping to create. But we know now that if you don't face the past you are condemned to be haunted by it. We have learned that it's best to honor the past by remembering it, and to not allow the horrific deeds of war to go unspoken, no matter how difficult it is to take in the knowledge. If we do not discuss the past, there are surely those who will take the opportunity to deny the truth and insist it never happened in the first place.

The remarkable book I found at a book fair opened up a world of grief and sorrow that I had never been told about before, but it also introduced me to the greatest first-person narrator in literature. For me, a working-class girl who had read only male writers in school, reading *The Diary of a Young Girl* was the first time that I realized that a young Jewish girl could be a writer. It was the book that made me want to become a writer, and it is highly unlikely that I would have ever imagined that as a possibility for myself had I not read Anne Frank's diary. A book belongs to its author, but it belongs to the reader as well, and a book can mean many things to many people. For me, *The Diary of a Young Girl* illuminated the desires of a girl who desperately wished to be a writer. Anne's voice spoke directly to me in a way no author had before. Despite the cruel ending of her life at the age of fifteen, her diary helped me to see that even when there was evil in the world, even when it was impossible to have hope, it was still possible to be brave. It was possible not to be forgotten and to live on in what you had written. It was possible to have a dream.

There are many reasons *The Diary of a Young Girl* is a classic and why Anne has become the voice of the Holocaust. Other families went into hiding, other people met with horrible, unfair fates, and other people wrote diaries documenting their experiences. Yet Anne's diary stands out, not just as a humanitarian document that reminds the world of what happened to the Jews and warns us about the rise of anti-semitism and the importance of attending to the needs of refugees, but also because it transcended its form to become true literature. It is Anne's singular voice, funny, annoying, and brilliant, which allows readers to feel that they know her. It is a voice so personal that when we read her diary we become Anne, and through her we experience a life we have never led. The book is both a warning and a blessing. What happened once can happen again. Evil does walk through the world, and it is often undetected until it's too late, as it was in the Netherlands and throughout Europe. As Anne writes letters in her diary to Kitty, her imaginary friend, we, the reader, become that friend, we are the person she is confiding in, the one who truly hears her, the one who learns lessons about love and remembrance.

No one knows what Anne's thoughts were before she began writing her diary, and much of her life between the ages of ten and thirteen is invented in the pages of my novel, including conversations and emotions and experiences. The details of relationships are imagined, though they are based on research and readings. There are characters and scenes that are invented as well, for it is impossible to know what went on day to day, what conversations people had with one another, and what their true feelings were. Writing historical fiction is much like writing a mystery—we must invent what we cannot know. We take pieces of history and re-create the world.

As far as we know, Anne's mother never gave her a necklace, and no one knows what Anne truly felt about Hello Silberberg, just as no one knows what discussions were had by the sisters, who were as different as day from night, but who were together until the very end of their lives. We do know that Anne had complicated relationships, especially with her mother and sister, and from onlookers' reports who were there when Edith and her daughters were sent to a camp together, and later when Margot and Anne were sent to yet another camp, it was said that they protected each other and spent all their time together, dying within days of each other.

The facts are the facts. The Netherlands was invaded on May 10, 1940, by Nazi Germany, which had already taken over Poland and Austria and whose mission was to rid the world of Jews, along with people of Slavic ancestry, the Roma and Sinti people, and others they thought not worthy of life, including gay men, lesbians, and transgender people, and the physically and mentally disabled. It is a fact that six million Jews died during the Holocaust, known also as the Shoah, the Hebrew word for catastrophe. It is a fact that three-quarters of Dutch Jews were murdered, the highest percentage of victims deported from a single country in western Europe, and one of the highest percentages of Jews killed in a single European country, said to be 102,000 victims. It is true that other countries turned Jewish refugees away, as refugees from brutal regimes continue to be turned away to this day. The Nazi philosophy was racist and antisemitic. Nazis believed the "Aryan" race, the Germans, were

AFTERWORD

superior. The Jews were seen as inhuman or as devils. Under the leadership of Adolf Hitler, the genocide of the Jews was the Nazi goal.

On August 4, 1944, Dutch police officers and an SS officer raided the Franks' hiding place and arrested the people in hiding and two of their helpers. The Frank family was put on the last train to Auschwitz from the Westerbork transit camp on September 3, 1944. Five hundred and forty-nine people were immediately taken from that transport to the gas chambers and murdered. Men and women were separated. Edith and her daughters were parted from Otto Frank on the train platform. Then the sisters were separated from Edith in November and transported to the Bergen-Belsen concentration camp. The liberation of the Netherlands by the Allies had begun that September, with the Canadian Army, including British and Polish units, being the first to fight the Nazis there, and soon American troops entered as well. But it was too late for the Franks by weeks or months. Edith Frank died in Auschwitz on January 6, 1945, three weeks before it was liberated. In Bergen-Belsen, typhus was everywhere, due to the horrendous conditions, and that contagious disease was the cause of thousands of deaths. Amsterdam was liberated on May 5, 1945. It is assumed that Anne Frank died from typhus, likely in February 1945, about two months before the Bergen-Belsen camp was liberated by British forces on April 15, 1945, and only a few days after her sister, Margot, died from the same disease. Otto survived, and one of Anne's close friends told me that when he returned to Amsterdam, every time he visited her, he was crying.

Anne was special, it's true, a brilliant writer and a lively mind, but she was also ordinary. In a way that is precisely what makes her so special to us. She was the girl we all are, lovable and exasperating and smart. She was a dreamer and a realist, but more than anything she was a girl who wanted a future. That is something she deserved, and when we remember her, and the fate of her people, we are honoring not only Anne, but all who were lost during the war. *Remember us*, the diary tells us, in every single line, which is why it should be required reading for every child in America and throughout the world. *Remember me.*

—Alice Hoffman

Acknowledgments

My extreme gratitude to my editors in New York and London, Lisa Sandell and Miriam Farbey, for bringing this project to me and having faith that together we could tell Anne's story during the years before the Frank family went into hiding. A special thanks to Lisa for all the hours we spent together. I could not have written this book without my editors, nor would I even have imagined doing so. Fiction is meant to make sense of a world that is so unbelievably cruel that sometimes we can only begin to understand the past and the present in the language of fairy tales and myths.

My gratitude to Amanda Urban for continuing to have faith, and to Ron Bernstein, who has always supported my work.

To my dear friend Jill Karp, love and gratitude for making the journey to Amsterdam with me.

All historical errors are mine alone, but I was fortunate to discuss the history of the Frank family with experts in Amsterdam. I am indebted to the Anne Frank House and to the researchers there who I was privileged to work with, Eugenie Martens, Menno Metselaar, and Gertjan Broek, as well as Tom Brink and Ronald Leopold. My deep thanks to Jacqueline van Maarsen and to Maarten Sanders for meeting with me.

Thank you also to Janny van der Molen and to Dienke Hondius for the conversation about Anne and the Frank family and the situation of those in hiding during the war.

Thank you to Rian Verhoeven for the tour of the Franks' neighborhood.

Thank you to Joan Adler at the Straus Historical Society.

Thank you to Madison Wolters and Deborah Revzin for their readings of the manuscript.

Thank you also to Professor Avinoam Patt, Doris and Simon Konover Chair of Judaic Studies and Director, Center for Judaic Studies and Contemporary Jewish Life,

University of Connecticut, for reading and fact-checking the manuscript.

Many thanks to Elizabeth Parisi and Seale Ballenger and to everyone at Scholastic. And thank you to Nicole Dewey.

To my grandmother Lillie, who told me her story of waking up with wolves and watching the birds in the forest, I will always be grateful.

Further Reading

Frank, Anne. *The Diary of a Young Girl*.
New York: Bantam Books, 1994.

Frank, Anne. *Tales from the Secret Annex*.
New York: Bantam Books, 2003

Metselaar, Menno. *Anne Frank, Dreaming, Thinking, Writing*.
Amsterdam: Anne Frank House, 2017.

Muller, Melissa. *Anne Frank, The Biography*.
New York: Henry Holt and Company, 2013.

About the Author

Alice Hoffman is the acclaimed author of over thirty novels for readers of all ages, including *The Dovekeepers*, *The World That We Knew*—winner of the Dayton Literary Peace Prize—*The Marriage of Opposites*, *Practical Magic*, *Incantation*, *The Foretelling*, and most recently, *The Invisible Hour*. Her previous novels for Scholastic Press are *Aquamarine*, which was made into a major motion picture, *Indigo*, *Green Witch*, and *Green Angel*, which *Publishers Weekly*, in a boxed, starred review, called "achingly lovely." She lives outside Boston. Visit her online at www.alicehoffman.com.

* * *

The Anne Frank House was established on May 3, 1957, in cooperation with Otto Frank, Anne Frank's father. They are an independent non-profit organization that runs a museum in the building where Anne Frank went into hiding, and they try to bring the life story of Anne Frank to the attention of as many people as possible worldwide, with the aim of raising awareness of the dangers of antisemitism, racism, and discrimination and the importance of freedom, equal rights, and democracy. The Anne Frank House researches the history of the Frank family and the other people in hiding, as well as antisemitism, racism, and right-wing extremism in the Netherlands.